The Quick-Change Artist

THE
QUICK-CHANGE
ARTIST

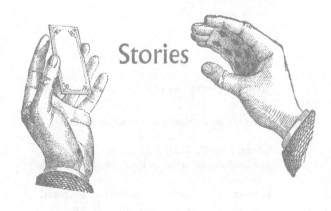

Stories

CARY HOLLADAY

Swallow Press / Ohio University Press   Athens, Ohio

Although John Cussons, Lizzie Fletcher, Polk Miller, and Edyth Beveridge were real people, they are depicted according to the author's imagination, and their representation is not intended as fact. All other characters are entirely the inventions of the author.

Swallow Press / Ohio University Press, Athens, Ohio 45701
www.ohio.edu/oupress

12 11 10 09 08 07 06   5 4 3 2 1

Library of Congress Cataloging-in-Publication Data

Holladay, Cary C., [date]
  The quick-change artist : stories / Cary Holladay.
    p. cm.
  ISBN-13: 978-0-8040-1092-4 (hardcover : alk. paper)
  ISBN-10: 0-8040-1092-7 (hardcover : alk. paper)
  ISBN-13: 978-0-8040-1093-1 (pbk. : alk. paper)
  ISBN-10: 0-8040-1093-5 (pbk. : alk. paper)
  1. City and town life—Virginia—Fiction. I. Title.

PS3558.O347777Q5 2006
813'.54—dc22

2006021271

Acknowledgments

The following were previously published, some in slightly different form.

"The Quick-Change Artist" as "The Green Children," *Black Warrior Review*

"The Peacock," *The North Atlantic Review*

"Heaven," *The Kenyon Review*

"The Blue Monkey," *Red Rock Review*

"The Lost Pony," "The Broken Lake," and "Jane's Hat," *Five Points*

"Syrup and Feather," *New Letters*

"Jane's Hat," *New Stories from the South: The Year's Best, 2005*

"The Iron Road," *Shenandoah*

"Sailor's Valentine," *The Southern Review*

"The Interview," *Blackbird: An Online Journal of Literature and the Arts*

"Snow Day," *The Idaho Review*

The author thanks the University of Memphis, the National Endowment for the Arts, the Tennessee Arts Commission, the Pennsylvania Council on the Arts, the Virginia Center for the Creative Arts, and the Corporation of Yaddo, all of which provided support during the creation of these stories.

"The Broken Lake" received the Paul Bowles Prize for Fiction from *Five Points*.

For Julie Mann and Hilary Holladay, my sisters,

and for George Holladay, our Daddy

Contents

The Quick-Change Artist

Forest Lodge
Glen Allen, Virginia
July 1928

VANGIE AND HER brother Luke are fishing at Hidden
Lake in the middle of the night. It's almost the same as day
for Luke, who is blind, totally and utterly, his eyeballs having
been removed long ago by Dr. Winfrey to prevent a fever and
infection from spreading to his brain.

To Vangie, Luke is a slim presence on the bank, a shadow
within darkness, casting out his line. They have done this many
times. Sometimes they swim, careful not to make noise, afraid
they'll be banished by the two sisters, Miss Amy and Miss
Dorothy, who own the five lakes and the hotel. In the distance, Vangie can see tiny lights: the flames of candles strapped
onto croquet wickets so hotel guests can play the game into
the night. She attached the candles herself, at Miss Amy's
direction.

"This lake's drying up," Luke says. "All of 'em are."

Vangie hardly hears him. She's lying on her back, propped up on her elbows. She's a chambermaid at the hotel. It's only because she's eighteen and in love that she can stay up half the night yet work the next day. She's in love with the magician who performs evenings and Saturday afternoons at the hotel. He is Vangie's lover, but she's afraid he might have other lovers, too. He's on her mind all the time, like a song.

Luke tugs at his line. He slips away often from the Home for the Blind, where he lives and goes to school, to visit with Vangie and their Grammah. He and Vangie have played in the hotel gymnasium at three in the morning, jumping rope, vaulting over a leather hurdle, swaying on rings suspended from the high ceiling, and swinging Indian clubs to make their arms strong. Now Luke brings in his fish, which flaps silver as he drags it through the water. He picks the hook out of its gills and sets it free. "I'm going soon," he says. "I'm sleepy."

"All right," Vangie says, wishing she were beautiful. She should go home herself, back to the little house where Grammah sleeps with her hair curled up in rags. If Vangie were beautiful, she believes, the magician, whose name is Jolly Erdos ("say air-dish," he always says) might train her to be a quick-change artist, waltzing onto the stage in a blue gown, then spinning once, twice, in the haze of smoke rising up in a scrim from the footlights, and lo and behold, she's wearing a yellow dress instead. Jolly has described quick-change but will not say how it's done. He will never tell his secrets. He calls tricks "effects." She has described the tricks to Luke, hoping he can figure them out, but he is baffled, too. Maybe it's impossible for a boy blind since age nine to picture a dogwood tree sprouting from a teacup in Jolly's hand, its limbs growing until it's a real tree, with buds unfurling into blossoms before the whole thing withers away, its limbs flopping over Jolly's arm. Then Jolly rolls it all up and stuffs it back into the teacup, covering it with a scarf. When he raises the scarf, a golden toad sits in the cup, breathing so that Vangie can see the motion of its tiny throat when Jolly strides to the edge of the stage.

Luke's face always glows when Vangie describes the toad. He has asked many questions: Does Jolly allow anybody to pet it? Does it try to hop away? Where did Jolly get it?

Luke is jostling Vangie's shoulder. Dew has crept through her dress to her skin, cool and damp. From the hotel yard, she hears the croquet players' laughter and the *thwack* of mallets striking balls. "I must've fallen asleep," she mumbles, rubbing her eyes.

"What are you going to do, Vangie?" Luke asks, as he has asked since they were little.

"What do you think? Go home. Go to bed."

"I mean forever. What'll you do?"

She wishes she were in bed already, with the sweet breeze blowing over the sheets. She picks out stars she knows: the Pleiades, a bright, blurred cluster so far away. She learned about stars from reading a book in the hotel library. "I wish I could marry Jolly," she says. There. She's kept it a secret from everybody, for so long, that now she feels a rush of joy just saying Jolly's name. She imagines Jolly as a farmer, right here in Glen Allen, pitching gold hay onto a wagon, and herself the farmer's bride.

Luke is silent for a while. "And then what?"

"I'd go to all the places he goes and help him with his shows. I help him already."

"With his clothes, you mean."

"Yes." It's her job to press the black swallowtail coat Jolly wears for performances, to shine his shoes and brush his top hat. Jolly made her promise not to examine the coat, but of course she has gone through every stitch and seam, finding only a few extra pockets where you might expect them to be, and they're always empty: not a coin or a feather. She has slipped the coat on over her dress, buttoned it debonairly, and swung her arms back and forth with a flourish so that its long tails part over her behind. She loves the smell of sweat that the ironing brings out. Jolly is not a big man, and the coat strains across her chest. She always irons the coat gently and stuffs the sleeves with paper. The other maids resent her for being chosen to take care of his room, his things. A colored girl gets to care for the rabbits and doves which he employs in his effects. The tiny golden toad lives in a bowl of water with pebbles to climb upon. The creatures are kept in clean cages on a sleeping porch off Jolly's third-floor room.

"Was it a full house tonight?" Luke asks, using a phrase they both relish.

"Oh yes," says Vangie. She stands up. "Afterwards, so many women were trying to get backstage that the sheriff had to block their way." She had thought that the sheriff was handsome; the thought was a betrayal of Jolly. As she and Luke turn away from the lake, she asks, "Where are you sleeping tonight?" Sometimes he sleeps in the woods. Vangie doesn't like to think of him out there, with the owls swooping over him, the trees so thick and dark. Dr. Winfrey and the headmaster at the Home for the Blind would be furious if they knew.

Even by moonlight, she can read the expression of his mouth, his forehead, cheeks, and dark glasses. He looks stubborn.

"Come on home," she says. "Grammah's got fresh eggs and butter. Breakfast will be so good. It's so dumb they make you stay at that school."

Grammah has fought with Dr. Winfrey about this. Dr. Winfrey insists that students live at the school, "for safety's sake," he says. Luke is the only local student. The others come from all parts of Virginia, from Roanoke, Winchester, Christiansburg, Culpeper. From Toano, Poquoson, Falmouth, Chatham. Many, like Luke, are poor, sent on a scholarship from a church. Luke's sponsor is Dr. Winfrey. Luke goes for free.

"I don't mind school that much," says Luke.

The hotel yard is empty when she and Luke reach it, the wicket candles burnt to nubbins. Vangie smells whiskey from the juleps the players drink. In the morning she'll find glasses with mint and melted ice stuck in the crotches of the oak trees.

"We're frying chicken tomorrow," she tells Luke, "for the parade. I'll bring you some." She reaches out to hug him goodnight. She knows he isn't coming home. When she embraces him, he's shaking, in deep, seismic waves.

"What's the matter?" She grips his arms. "Are you sick? Oh Luke, come on home. It's too hot to sleep in the woods, and won't the skeeters be bad?"

"I'm fine," he says, and the shaking calms. He reaches in his pocket and pulls out some money. "Give this to Grammah," he says. He makes a little money caning chairs. The Home for the Blind has a workshop where the best students get to learn caning and piano tuning. There's even an airy, high-ceilinged studio for sculpting, complete with a potter's wheel.

Vangie takes the money. Luke turns from her, and then she's alone on the path going back to her house. She looks back but doesn't see him. Only once did he let her examine the pits where his eyes used to be. His easy getting around always astonishes Vangie, Grammah, and everybody else. No cane: he can sense when the way is clear, he always says, and when it's not.

She's so tired that she's falling asleep already, though she's on her feet and walking the half-mile back to her house. She bets Jolly's still awake, lying flat on his bed with his bright black eyes open in the darkness. It's a torment to wonder if she's just his daytime girl and he has others at night. It's his stories that have reeled her in, more than passion itself: stories of his gypsy life, strange and brilliant as lightning, and the magic, which she would love to learn.

Then her vision turns ghastly. She sees Jolly dying, burning inside out with fever, his swallowtail coat flung off and crumpled on the floor like a crow. She sees Dr. Winfrey baffled, checking Jolly's pulse while he times it on his gold pocket watch. Jolly's chin juts out as if he's jumping off a cliff. His eyes are closed, and he is sunken into himself.

In terror, she plunges forward on the path. The harder she fights the picture, the clearer it is, as if she is watching the scene right in front of her. She smells a salty odor like the scent of the seashells he uses in some of his tricks, only stronger. Maybe it's the smell of tears, her own and other women's. The vision brings her the hotel yard full of parked automobiles, silent with their headlamps on, and in every car is a woman, weeping, waiting for news.

She bursts through the door of her house. Grammah never locks it. She thinks she will faint, or vomit. In bed, she prays to push the vision away. She falls asleep fighting it.

FORTY CHICKENS to cut up and fry, six pans of cobbler to bake. Miss Amy, the older and wilder of the two sisters who own the hotel, is talking about breasts. "She's got pendulums," she says, pointing to her sister Dorothy, "and I've got fried eggs."

Vangie laughs. She has never heard anybody talk the way Miss Amy does. Her pretty sister, Miss Dorothy, is always pouting and put-upon. Dorothy likes to remind everybody that she is a widow, her sister an old maid. Before they came here from Worcester, Massachusetts, and bought the hotel from a man named Claude Revelle, they had never been to the South.

"Faithless and mean, every one of 'em," Miss Amy says of the men she has loved. Her cleaver comes down smartly on a chicken back, splitting it.

"I shouldn't have to do this!" Miss Dorothy complains.

"We all have to work," her sister says. "Even you, Miss High and Mighty."

Miss Amy has corralled chambermaids, washerwomen, and cooks, ten women including herself and her sister. Each must cut up four chickens. Vangie doesn't mind. Miss Amy made them all wash their hands in front of her, in the big sink. The head cook is dumping flour and cornmeal into a big bowl, her brown arm shining as she shakes salt into the mixture.

"It's an easy life," Miss Amy declares, her cleaver flashing, "when all you have to do is chop four chickens."

The old veterans, who will eat the chicken, are already gathered in the parlor. They're making a day of it, with lectures in the morning. The first is on "Progress on Wartime Diseases," given by Dr. Winfrey. Vangie finishes cutting up her chickens and goes to lean close to the parlor door, hearing the words *erysipelas, gangrene, pyaemia, dysentery.* Dr. Winfrey asks the men what other ills they suffered in the war, and Vangie hears a chorus of barks and creaks as respondents call out *catarrh, mumps! Scrofula, camp itch, measles, typhoy!*

It has been sixty-three years since the Civil War. Vangie wonders how it feels to be as old as the veterans, to have fought and to have had those diseases, to have lived through other wars since then. Grammah was born the year the war ended.

A stock-and-bond broker from Richmond will give the second talk of the day, "Investing to Make the Most of Your Money." The broker waits on a settee in the hallway, fussing with papers. He tells Vangie, "Bring me a Coca-Cola, coldest you've got."

Vangie welcomes the chance to stick her arm deep into the frosty bin in the back of the kitchen. The cold air swirls up into her hair. She lifts out a bottle, uncaps it, and takes it to the man in the hall. Miss Amy's already there, snapping a nickel out of the man's fingers.

"I'm a damyankee," Miss Amy says. "I count every cent."

The man stares at her open-mouthed. She sits down beside him and says, "Now tell me about these investments of yours."

Vangie can't help but chuckle. In her head, she's always marrying people off, coupling them like dolls: Miss Amy and this stockbroker, never mind that he's years younger than she is; Miss Dorothy and Mr. Shippen, a lawyer who helped arrange the sale of the hotel; or maybe Miss Dorothy and Dr. Winfrey. Dr. Winfrey, a widower, lives at the hotel.

She hasn't seen Jolly today. He usually sleeps late. She guesses that he was one of the croquet players last night, with a beautiful, scandalous woman named Helen Revelle, whose husband sold the hotel to Miss Amy and Miss Dorothy. Helen Revelle and her husband are divorced, and Helen rents a large suite at the hotel. Vangie knows that if Jolly falls in love with Helen Revelle, she may as well give up. She can never compete with a black-haired beauty who spent months in a Kentucky cave being cured of TB. She loves to hear Helen talk about the patients in their nightclothes, in their beds far underground, taunting the tourists in headlamps and cave-crawling boots: "Welcome to hell. Pull up a bed and stay a while!"

Vangie feels sluggish from the heat and sick from love. A thousand thoughts of Jolly are making her sick. She looks for him on the porch. Often he's there in a rocking chair, holding court, but not today. She might go knock on his door. That was how they started, when she knocked and he invited her in and offered her round yellow sweets from Spain.

"These are *yemas*," he had said, "made of candied egg yolk and lemon."

The candy tasted sour and strange. She spat it into her hand, and Jolly laughed. He dragged a trunk from his closet and lifted several jars from it, jars containing horrible slimy snakelike creatures that pressed against the glass, thin whitish ribbons or thick gray coils with suction cups. He said they were tapeworms which he got at a stockyard. He said, "I used to claim they'd been taken out of people's stomachs, and then I'd sell them a jar of special tonic." He laughed, then reached for Vangie and kissed her with light, stinging kisses while his birds whirred on the sleeping porch, lively silhouettes with fanlike wings.

She decides she won't go to his room, now. She has always been the one to knock; he has not even had to come looking for her, and afterward, she always rises from his bed and goes back to work, while he stays there sleeping.

Already, people are crowding onto the hotel verandah, staking out rocking chairs and railings as the best seats from which to watch the parade. The old Confederates will march and then eat their fried chicken. They'll have the cobbler too, and pimento cheese sandwiches, potato salad, devil's food cake, and lemonade.

Chicken: the glorious fried scent leads Vangie back to the kitchen. Not until she gets Miss Amy's permission does she put some into a basket covered with a towel. Miss Amy has a soft spot for Luke.

Walking up Mountain Road, she eats a drumstick, tossing the bone into the ditch and licking her fingers. She can see the glimmer of Castle Lake from the road. What was it Luke said about the lakes drying up? She pictures them parched to deep cups, filled with leaves, rustling and sifting, swallowing her up as she struggles to swim through the leaves, dry leaves crawling with spiders and ready to catch on fire. Her mother and father died in a fire soon after Luke was born. Vangie is terrified of fire. She burned a pan of popcorn one time and screamed so loud, the neighbors came. Her father gave her her fanciful name: Evangeline, after a long-ago girl who lived in the woods.

It's fear she feels as the chicken bone settles down in the hissing ditch, grasshoppers and katydids crying out around her and springing up in the dry field grass. She cut her hand on ditch grass once, reaching for a piece of shiny tin. The grass was knife-sharp; her blood was red script on her palm. She was amazed: cut not by tin but by grass.

Fear, and why? She's in love, she's got fried chicken for her brother, and there will be a parade to celebrate the Fourth of July, though the old men say they're remembering Gettysburg, and never mind that they lost.

The Home for the Blind sits on a low rise, plain as a jail.

He's not in the dormitory, the long room with the bunk beds; not in the classroom where students look up from their Braille spellers when she knocks on the door and steps inside with her voice rising; not in workshop or studio, kitchen or yard.

"We haven't seen him since yesterday," the children tell her. The teacher says, "We thought he was with you and your Grammah."

The headmaster comes out of his office. "I have called the sheriff," he says.

They're all staring at her. Nobody can stare like a blind child.

"We have to go through this place from top to bottom," Vangie says and is amazed when they do it—teacher, headmaster, students from the tiny ones to those nearly grown. The students search by calling and feeling, patting the Home down like Grammah pats pie dough. No Luke, though feathers flutter from turned-over mattresses and the hallways echo with the thumps of closet doors flung wide.

The sheriff arrives, a young man with blue eyes whose face looks like he is about to laugh, but his words come out serious. To Vangie, he says, "I remember you from the show last night. Isn't that something, how women go for that little foreign fellow! Now when did you last see your brother?"

"We went fishing last night," she says.

She realizes her hands are empty. Where did she put that basket of fried chicken? She must have set it down when they all searched the school. They're in the studio with her—sheriff, headmaster, students, two teachers. Somebody has sculpted a mermaid, white plaster with a chunky, scaly tail, painted green. It has breasts. Vangie can't believe this was allowed here, the making of this beautiful creature with breasts that look so real. Its head has plaster ringlets of hair. She gazes from the mermaid to the sheriff and says, "What if somebody took my brother?"

"A kidnapping?" The sheriff's eyebrows shoot up. "Have you gotten a ransom note?"

"No," Vangie says, floundering. "What if he drowned?"

"We'll drag the lakes," the sheriff says, "but not till we search at your Grammah's house."

The headmaster looks at her keenly and says, "He ran off, didn't he. Does he dislike it here?"

She's glad she's able to tell him, "He doesn't mind it. He said so." She herself has lain on Luke's bunk bed during visiting hours, testing it out, seeing how it feels to lie so close to the ceiling, to imagine sleeping among so many others in the long, narrow dormitory.

She feels sick with fear and dread, but she only wants him to be happy. *Run, Luke, run. Oh Luke, run, run . . .* The blind students, surrounding her, are radiant with borrowed adventure.

"We'll find him," the sheriff declares and then says, as if to himself, "Who could ever believe this, that a boy with no eyes could run away?" He tells Vangie to get in his car, that he will drive her home. Why, he bets they will find Luke there.

The sheriff's car is a wonder, swift and black, and he drives too fast. When Vangie hangs her arm out the window, the wind burns it. She hears some kind of commotion and opens her mouth to ask the sheriff if he hears it too, but he's frowning at the road, all haste and hurry.

They turn the corner onto Mountain Road and run smack into the old men's parade, hurtling right into the marching column. Vangie feels the bump of bodies, sees men tossed sideways like crabs, rolling away from the car. The old soldiers buck and yell. The sheriff stands on his brakes, and Vangie screams. The car stops so hard she falls forward, hitting her head. For a moment, she doesn't hear anything, and then sounds come faintly, growing louder as she opens her eyes.

All around her, the old men are firing rifles and pistols into the air. She feels a hand on her arm, feels herself being turned around in the seat and lifted out so she can stand. Dust rises curtain-like around the car. Somewhere, horses are whinnying. She can't see; the sun's brilliant in her eyes. The sheriff is beside the car, hollering. Who was it who lifted her out of the car? A man steps forward, an old man in a gray jacket and cavalry pants. A drum beats, a cornet blares, somebody's honking the horn of the sheriff's car, on and on and on, and somehow all of it makes a tune.

The old man speaks: "Would you dance with me, miss?"

He reaches for her hands and puts them on his shoulders. His uniform feels soft as moths beneath her palms, but he's strong. They whirl in the dust while others cheer. She hears a gleeful voice call, "Nobody's killed, Sheriff! Don't you worry!"

The old man is light on his feet, and she follows his steps, dancing some reel in the road. She remembers dancing with her mother as a tiny girl, when her mother taught her how to clean a room: you do your end and I'll do mine, and we'll twirl when we meet in the middle.

Old soldiers are pressing close and clapping as her partner spins her round and round. Her hair comes loose and spills to her waist. She's thinking: Let me go, for I am wasting time. But if he lets her go, she'll shoot like a coiled spring, flying away. She thinks she hears Miss Amy's cleaver fall, sees through the aching sunlight a floating milkweed puff which catches on her cheek and stays there through the whirling. Luke was how far away by the time Miss Amy's cleaver fell, and how much farther now? He will go to the ocean. He will run to the docks. That basket of chicken: where now? Somebody'll find it and eat it, some blind child; she hopes that's what will be and not ants and flies devouring it. Ants and flies: but she's dancing a hundred miles an hour, a dreidl, can't think for moving. She hears laughter, her own. Jolly has spoken of his childhood, of tossing dreidls in the air, singing with his family, picking the pockets of those who gathered to watch the musicians and the dreidl-throwing, a small dark boy with busy fingers digging the money out. Gold coins, he said, and silver. His parents taught him. He snickered, describing this: a thief, and she hates thieving.

Like jumping Johnnies, the men struck by the sheriff's car leap to their feet, brushing themselves off, their yells dying to hot spit in their throats. They stomp the ground, shouting, hoarse in the dryness, while she and the old dancing soldier turn to cyclones, dust devils in the road. Behind them, the train comes, its noise shutting out all the other sounds so that her ears hold only a ringing, hollow silence. Will she never see this man's face. Hair in her eyes, sun in her eyes, thirsty, her feet drumming the road, a breakneck gallop mile by mile, all in this little space. She hears Luke cry, *Hot pepper,* and his jumprope flails. Luke, come home. Come home and pet your tortoiseshell cat, the one the bluejays hector, the one that licks her pretty paws. *I'll never get over what Dr. Winfrey did.* Her breath's gone, laughter gone, her legs are hammers, the old man grasps her hands so tight she'll have to let them go, he'll slide her arms off her like sleeves. Sick at her stomach when Grammah told her: *Took out his eyes.* Grammah's wild, clawing at her hair, all in a stagger and a frenzy: *Took out his eyes and sewed 'em shut.*

HE EMERGES as a suitor: the old man. "Marry me," he says the very next day, as she sits on a stump in Grammah's yard and he stands ramrod-straight before her. "You will get the pension. Other girls have done just this same thing."

"But you're older than my Grammah," she says, as dazed as she was when they danced.

"I don't look so old, do I?" he says, and with his proud stance and the sun behind him, she can't see the wrinkles in his shadowed face. His abundant hair is the color of light, combed in the long Western way down the back of his neck, and yes, he does look young from where she sits on the rough stump, with the sun in her eyes. He says, "I can help you find your brother. I have friends who are policemen and inventors. One is working on a device that seeks out human heat from the air. Someday, he'll get it right, and it'll pick out a person even in the dark or in the woods, finding them from their body heat as sure as a cat leaves a warm spot on a bed. What I wouldn't give to have it ready for you."

Nobody has ever wanted to give her such a thing, and her heart leaps at it, sinks again, comes back to the single truth. "But you're way up in years. I mean no disrespect. You must have children who are old too, and grandchildren about my Grammah's age."

"My folks are gone," he says, "but I've got some buddies alive to march with and a good many years ahead of me. What if I were young? Would you let me court you then, or do you love somebody else?"

"He doesn't love me back." She hears the birds' wings whirring, tries to feel Jolly's arms around her, but all she recalls is the tightness of his swallowtail coat, when she has tried it on.

"It's the sheriff, isn't it," the old man says, smacking his fist into his palm, "even though he can't drive worth a damn."

"Not the sheriff," Vangie says, her breath quickening flame-like in her throat as she yearns for Jolly.

"So you say," he says, relaxing a little, rocking on his heels, and she sees how he might have leaned against a rail fence beside a battlefield, oh, years ago, all springing step and keen-eyed leisure, waiting for the smoke to clear and the last Yankees to retreat, while he knuckled the black powder from his eyes. "The way you rode in the sheriff's car, with your arm out the window for the breeze: that looked to me like you belonged to him."

"It's Jolly Erdos," she blurts. "The magician. But he has so many women in love with him. They give him presents and money."

"Can he drive a car without hitting a whole parade?" The old man throws back his head and laughs.

"I have these bad thoughts about him, like dreams or bad miracles. I see him dying."

He reaches out and touches her cheek. His hand is soft and does not shake. He says, "How long now since your brother's been gone? About two days?"

"He's fine, I know it. The sheriff dragged the lakes today and didn't find him."

"I was blind during the war," he says, "but only at night. It was scurvy. A whole corps of us were sick that way and had to be led around by the hand after dark. But in the day, we kept on fighting."

She's embarrassed yet proud when Miss Amy says, "You've got Major *Raymond* interested in you," in a scolding tone, which shows that she's impressed. And Grammah says, "Honey, you're an orphan, and I won't live forever," to which Vangie says, "Aren't I supposed to notice that he's about a hundred?"

"He's still good-looking," Grammah says. "He's the youngest old fellow I've ever seen."

Old as he is, does he still count as a suitor? Vangie feels mean-spirited for wondering. Yes, other girls have married old men, yet their reasons are always suspect, tainted. Her vanity's the quick-change artist; one minute she's queenly, the next she's appalled, for he is just too old. But who is she to send him away? She's a chambermaid, and he is a major. She had never noticed him before they danced in the road, though she knew his name, the way she knew the names of Mountain Road and North Run Creek and of his farm, Sunning Hill.

He named the place for his wife, who sunned herself there on the lawn while the house was being built, fifty years ago. His wife used to sit beneath a tent made of canvas and armchairs while carpenters hammered and whistled, and in the late afternoon she would step out of the tent, lie down on the grass, and sleep.

How quiet it is in the Major's house, though Vangie senses eyes upon her, for he has servants to polish his mahogany sideboards and dust his porcelain figurines, servants who must be hiding behind the painted Oriental screens and potted ferns. Proudly, the Major shows her a gallery of photographs: there he is with other men having supper at a table crowded with candelabra and silver platters, their heads crowned with wreaths.

"Don't we look silly," the Major says, leaning over her shoulder. "That's how you get gout. That was the nineties, all excess and pride."

And there's the sunning wife on that very lawn that Vangie sees out the window, a green lawn rendered in black and white in the photograph. She's young, sprawling on her back in a long dress, holding an infant high above her, laughing. The child's head blocks out the sun so that its rays fan out around the bright filaments of his hair.

"This would all be yours," the Major says. Vangie hears the words as if she's dreaming them. She and Grammah are in the Major's library, on a day so hot that ghosts of heat shimmer above the green grass beyond the windows. He tells her, as if Grammah's not even there (avid, too excited to sip her glass of sweet tea), "You don't have to love me."

Yesterday, sitting on the stump, she'd believed that the pension he spoke of was what he would give to her, and that had not been of any interest to her. The very word *pension* sounds paltry to her, a trickle, something squeezed out of sorrow and want. This estate, this bounty, is too much. She and Grammah are accustomed to meals of batterbread and plain fish. Here, there would be Christmas food year round.

She gazes into the Major's face, searching for the young person who aged into this one, sensing kindness has always resided in his heart. "Why me?" she says, humble enough to wonder. She's only asking.

He takes that as a "yes," lifts her hand to his lips and kisses it, his mustache grazing her knuckles. "My dear," he says, "I've waited all my life for you. You're so beautiful, and you dance like you're on fire. You don't see how fine you are."

She had not meant yes, but now it's too late. She has never been so hugely misunderstood, and her jaw drops as Grammah, behind the old man's back, raises both her arms in triumph, her worn face a study in glee.

"You won't change your mind, now, will you?" the Major says. "Young girls are always hoping for better. Waiting and dreaming." And he shakes his head. "I had enough of that, oh plenty of that, back when I fought in the war."

"A FRIEND of mine loved violets so much that her whole wedding was made out of them," says Helen Revelle that afternoon, working on Vangie's hair, cutting it short and sleek like her own. "She had violets twined on the banister, violets in the chandelier, violets in the bridesmaids' sashes, even though it was wintertime. Her mother and father had violets shipped in from wherever they grew."

Swaths of Vangie's cut hair lie across her feet like dozing minks. She kicks them away and tosses her head, loving the fresh windy feeling around her neck. Since Luke disappeared, she has lain awake with her long, hot hair strangling her. Grammah believes he is dead. She says he'll be found in the woods some day, curled up and cold, and then she cries.

Smiling her beautiful smile, Helen says, "You'll have a place in society now. Your short hair won't get in the way of the games you'll play. You should take lessons in tennis and golf."

But it was enough to swing the Indian clubs with Luke in the hotel gym, her muscles tight as a bow-and-arrow. *Run, Luke, run, get where you want to go.* She's had moments of forgetting Luke. She has been distracted by the Major, while Luke is maybe not eating or sleeping; he might be wandering in confusion in some strange place, unable to make people understand who he is. She hates herself for taking the money he gave her that night at the lake.

"Major Raymond will buy you a car," Helen goes on, "a convertible, and you can learn to drive. You can go to horse shows. You can go to Hot Springs, with the Major or without him. I'll go with you. I love it there."

Vangie sees herself driving an open car, goggles over her eyes, a scarf on her head. No more ironing Jolly's coat. She's a maid no longer, can't believe she's being treated like a friend by Helen Revelle, Helen who muses: "The day my husband sold the hotel was the day our divorce came through. I sat with him in this hotel parlor while he sold it to Amy and Dorothy.

He was drunk as hell, and so was their lawyer." She laughs, drawing the brush through Vangie's hair, and goes on, "It was fall, warmer outside than inside, and the leaves were coming down fast. In the hour it took to sign the papers, the leaves piled up higher than the wheels of my car. But I hadn't been out of the cave very long, and the whole world looked beautiful then."

"I have to tell Jolly," Vangie says, to Helen and to this short-haired stranger in the mirror, "tell him about the Major."

"I told him. He's happy for you. He'll still have me. Here, try my lipstick. There's no little gypsy baby on the way, is there?"

"No." She turns and confronts Helen Revelle. "You should have let me tell him myself."

"Jolly said your brother's done the greatest trick of all, a blind boy disappearing. What color did his eyes used to be?"

She has to remember a long way, to bring that back, and then the image of his child-face with hazel eyes intact almost makes her cry. "I've got to go look for him. Nobody's looking." Yet she just stands there, gazing at herself in the mirror, her reflection diamond-sharp.

"Be my guest," Helen says. "Listen," she says. "When I was in the cave, I fell in love. He and I used to paint each other's teeth with stuff that glowed in the dark, and then we'd pace away from each other and see how far apart we could be and still see each other smile. It was so dark, his smile was all I could see."

Vangie can't help but ask, "What happened to him?"

Helen shrugs, taking the lipstick from Vangie's hand and leaning toward the mirror to use it. "I don't know. He might still be down there. He might be dead."

"How could you leave, when you loved him?"

"You're thinking how mean I am. You're thinking you'd have stayed," Helen says, "but you wouldn't have."

"WHAT HAVE you done?" cries Grammah, her hands flying to her mouth. "Hair chopped off and paint on your lips. Does the Major know about this?"

"Here he comes," Vangie says, seeing the tall, straight figure pegging toward the door. "We're going to the magic show. I just came back so you could see my hair."

"Don't run him off, child," Grammah says.

"What about Luke?" Vangie says, her voice rising to a shout. "Don't forget about him, Grammah, just because of the Major."

"Maybe he'll hear about you getting married and come on home," Grammah says, in a voice too hearty for truth. "We might get a letter or a telegram. Why, there's a telephone at Sunning Hill. He'll call you and be so proud you married Major Raymond."

Vangie opens the door and greets the Major, but her mind is on Luke and Jolly. Is she really surprised about Helen, or is the dust in her throat only from the dry evening and the effort of walking home from the hotel and now back again with the Major, who says it's too nice out to take the car? He says, "I'll test myself and you. I'll be watching you while the magician puts on his show."

She says, "I don't want you getting tired." It's how she would talk to a grandfather if she had one, yet this is the man she will marry. The Major buys the tickets and leads her to a seat in the auditorium. She feels people watching them, gossiping about the chambermaid who turned an old man's head, marrying him for his money, and she wants to yell, "It's not that way!"

There's Jolly, up on stage, but the lights are on him and the audience sits in near-darkness, so she knows he can't see her. The Major whispers that he likes her hair short. May he hold her hand? His hand feels as strong as a young man's and she thinks, He'll take care of Grammah and me. When she pictures living at Sunning Hill, she feels the way she did when she fell off the suspension rings in the hotel gym one night and lay with the wind knocked out of her. The Major is spry and clean, and his skin still fits him well, but she can't imagine how long his life has been, and here she is at the tail end of it, with him saying he's waited all those years for her. Pity fills her, pity for his tumultuous heart.

Jolly's got something new in his act: ventriloquism. He makes a teakettle talk, makes songs come from a fat man's stomach, and carries on a funny, rude conversation with a corner of the ceiling.

"He won't stay in Glen Allen," the Major whispers. "He'll go to big cities and make lots of money. He has stayed here because of you."

"Just try to enjoy the show," Vangie whispers back.

"Promise me you won't go to him any more."

She wants to agree, to make him happy, but grief rises like floodwater in her heart.

"I'll put him on the next train out of town. I won't have him near you," the Major says in a voice loud enough to lead a cavalry charge. "We'll be married tomorrow."

"Hush! Would y'all be quiet," hisses a woman beside them, a harsh whiff of tobacco on her breath. Vangie looks at the Major, but it's so dark, all she can make out is the shape of his shoulder. If Jolly can make a tree grow in a teacup, then she can learn to love the Major.

Jolly holds a hoop of fire while a little dog hops through it. He will tell a story of his childhood, he says, and Vangie could swear he looks straight at her over the footlights. He says, "Farmers were reaping in the fields when a little boy and girl came climbing out of pits where wolves were thought to live. They were wild, these children, with green skin and green clothes. Yes, green skin, and they spoke a strange language. The farmers took them into town and showed them to the others. They would eat only beans and water. After many months, they were able to say they'd been lying in a valley in their homeland when they heard lovely music and were transported to those fields."

Back and forth leaps the dog. Moments ago, he was a spotted puppy; by jumping through the ring of fire, he has grown into a setter with long red fur. "This happened in my village in the Old Country," Jolly goes on, a droll droop to his mouth. "So these green children were baptized, but the boy died. The girl lived to grow up. The green faded from her skin, and she got married just like any other girl in the village. She's beautiful, and her children are happy."

Jolly blows on the blazing hoop and the fire sizzles out, leaving pink smoke. The dog leans against his knee. The auditorium is quiet for an instant, then people clap and whistle. Even the Major is on his feet, applauding. Women rise from their seats and charge toward the small man in the swallowtail coat, who doffs his top hat and turns to run, just as the lights come up.

"I'll rip off his clothes if I get him alone," says the tobacco-breathed woman beside Vangie. "I'll make parts of *him* talk, all right," and the woman flashes lean, hairy calves as she hikes up her skirt and leaps onto the stage.

Behind Vangie, a man laughs, the sound rich and relaxed over the din. It's the sheriff. He leans over Vangie's shoulder to say, "I've given up protecting him. He's the luckiest damned man on Earth. I love this show and the ruckus after, love it."

The Major sighs and sinks into his seat, his cheeks showing a grape-colored flush. He says, "I can't imagine how those tricks are done, and I liked the story. I concede that much."

She lays her hand against the Major's face. He is burning up. She feels his wrist, finds a light, unruly pulse in his veins, and turns to the sheriff to say, "He's sick. Get the doctor."

People swoop down on them. Vangie fans the Major's face with her palm. By the time Dr. Winfrey bumbles in with his black bag, the Major is dead, a lock of long hair falling over his forehead, her old bridegroom and cavalier.

THE SHERIFF's two dogs, King Dan and Rebel Sue, sniff the shirt Vangie hands them—Luke's shirt—and take off, lolloping so low to the ground they might be plowing with their noses. They snuffle and tumble down the hill from the Home for the Blind and follow a path along the woods.

"They've picked up cold trails before," says the sheriff with pride. "I wish I'd done this the day your brother took off. When I ran into that parade, it knocked the wits right out of me."

"I've got to look for him. I've waited too long already. But I don't have much time," Vangie says. There's the funeral to go to, the Major's funeral, where she'll wear a black veil Grammah made for her. The world will pass through the parlor at Sunning Hill to say good-bye to him. She was too late in coming to him, in being found by him, and she's late again, for the funeral is now. She had the veil over her face when the sheriff came with his dogs and said they would look for Luke. She set the veil aside, though Grammah wrung her hands.

"Oh, we've got enough time," the sheriff says, guiding her toward the sound of the dogs. "I saw that magician getting on the train. He said it's bad luck if anybody dies at a show. That Mrs. Revelle went with him. They deserve each other, those two."

"What about the birds? The critters he used in his shows, did he take them too?"

The sheriff grins. "They were traveling light. Why, you want that trick toad?"

"My brother likes it. I want it for him." It's a misty morning, yet she detects some movement in the trees up ahead, where the dogs are, and she squints, pointing. "Look."

The sheriff says, "They found something, all right. They're going wild."

"Luke!" she says, straining her eyes for a human shape. It's too much to lose them all at once, Luke and the Major and Jolly. "I didn't try hard enough."

"Who ever does?" the sheriff says, as if she's making sense. "Well, I don't see anybody, but we'll catch up with the dogs. Might be just a possum."

"He said he was sleepy," she says with a shock of happiness. Weren't his last words about sleep? She should have known all along that he lay down in the woods and is only now waking up. He'll be hungry, brushing leaves out of his hair and yawning. She makes herself walk slowly beside the sheriff so she can believe it, for this one step and then another. *I have so much to tell you.* The sheriff slips his arm around her waist, warm and easy, like it belongs there.

The Peacock

SHE WAS BORN a long time ago, on a day when the bugs chewed the grape leaves into lace. Her mother in labor claimed to hear a rose by her bedside singing, swore that the rose was smiling even though you couldn't see the smile. Why don't more women talk about that, the mother said, that when you give birth your senses grow a thousand times. The name that she gave her daughter was Lila.

This is how Lila lives now: in the old hotel with its white paint peeling off in ribbons, exposing gray patches of weathered wood. The big lodge was built in the 1880s; when the hotel's walls were trees, the dying out of the Indians had not been too long a time before. Many years have passed. The lodge isn't beautiful anymore, unless you think vast disrepair is lovely. Its four stories stand as tall as the giant oaks in the yard; one of its two towers is gone. Laundry billows from its balconies. Lila lives on the third floor, in a corner room. Beside the hotel runs a road. At one time it was a dirt path. In the thirties, it was paved and a sign put up to name it officially what it had been called for more than two hundred years: Mountain Road. Land is flat here, just over the fall line, but if you stay on the road and go west about eighty miles, you'll be in the mountains. The road will take you there, just as it has taken travelers for a long time.

So there's the huge obsolete old hotel, with the road beside it, and just in front of it, incredibly close, the railroad tracks. You're a seven-year-old girl in the community; it's the mid-sixties. You have walked the half mile from your house to the one-story brick grocery store that sits on Mountain Road just opposite the old hotel. You have come here for the complicated thrill of buying a candy bar, of seeing the train go past (Chessie System, C&O, RF&P, Southern . . . so loud you close your eyes and lean your elbows on a big stack of dog food bags outside the store and just swim with the glory of the train), and finally, for the hope of glimpsing Lila and gleaning a little more of the mystery of who she is and what she did. You run as close to the tracks as you dare, to wave to the man in the caboose. The train makes you wild—happy and sad at the same time. You eat the candy bar, sucking the chocolate off the coconut, and stare up at the hotel's window till your neck hurts. A pigeon visits a high balcony rail, its red feet snapping (you squint to make sure the feet are red; your eyes are that sharp). A car or two passes by. The town, Glen Allen, is too small to be called a town. It's just a place, a crossroads. The grocery store and the old hotel are the "downtown." Behind the hotel are deep woods. Mountain Road crosses the tracks. The village has a few houses on the road and a few side streets, and more forest.

That pigeon on the balcony—tail up, it flips a white dropping into the air, and you smile.

Then you hear something, a high knocking throat rattle, and you're alert. Not ten yards away, across the tracks, a peacock fans all his feathers into glory, the eyes on his gleaming blue feathers gazing with the deep shallow stare of the faces in a deck of cards. His small head lifts toward you. He shakes his tufted crown. The bright display grows and grows, so that you see all sorts of colors in the feathers, green and red and white and brown, a wizard's palette, the first such bird you've ever seen.

The train comes swiftly. Why didn't you hear its whistle, its early rumbles? It shoots between you and the peacock. Oh boy, passenger cars: low green windows with the reading heads lined up, the reading important heads that sometimes turn into faces, smiling at you for half a heartbeat. Coal cars. Lumber. Caboose.

The tracks are still vibrating when you step across them to look for a blue feather, an elegant avian footprint. But the peacock is gone. The woods tell you nothing. The clearing, just in front of them, is empty.

It was all because of a man, of course—John Cussons—and if you'd been living back then you'd have known the power of that name. Everything that happened was because of John Cussons and the way he and Lila were together. And Susan Sheppard, John's wife. Lila is the only one still alive. Death has forgotten to come get her, and now she is a hundred years old. Death has not taken her by age or disease or accident or any other thing that ends a life. God gave her a long life to think about how she came between a man and his wife. If you stood outside the old hotel, you could feel her thinking their names: John and Susan. John. And Susan again.

This is how the story goes, from way back. John Cussons came to Glen Allen, and as long as he was here, this was the place to be, even if the summers were hot and filled with bugs and the winters were raw. He was the kind of man that people talked about. If you were a woman, you were thrilled by him in a secret way. There was something about the way his eyes were set in his face that made you stare at him, something about the shoulders that made you want to run your hand over them and feel the muscles, trace your fingers down his chest and get lost in what happened next. When you talked with him, you longed to be alone with him. Then he smiled, and you woke from your dream, dry-mouthed, heart leaping, hands hanging limp at your sides.

He wore his dark hair long and his long beard full, and he still had the boots he'd worn to fight for the South twenty years before, when he was first a scout and then in the trenches at Fort Mahone. Fort Damnation, the men called it. When people wanted to talk about Cold Harbor and Yellow Tavern and all those battles around Richmond and Petersburg, about the mud and the cannon fire and the men ripped open right next to you—when somebody wanted to talk about the war, John Cussons grew quiet, and soon you found you were talking about something else.

He bought this land after the war, a thousand acres with mineral springs that seemed to him like paradise. The land was flat, and after a rain it sparkled with puddles under the tall stretched-out pines and oaks. He cleared the land himself. He married Susan Sheppard, who was said to be beautiful, though today no photographs of her exist. And for a brief time, Lila, who was much younger than they were, intruded in their lives, and she outlived them both.

Now people ask Lila's advice about love. They climb the stairs to her apartment, knock at the door, and cock their heads, listening for the whisper of her slippers on the floor. Usually she doesn't answer. But now and then she lets someone in, and the visitor asks a question or two about love as if Lila is some kind of oracle, before throwing their heart in with someone else's. Why? Lila never goes out; it's not as if she knows everybody. But she knows what's past. She herself, a living secret, must know the secrets of others.

YOUR FATHER died two years ago, when you were five. It was some bad disease that had to do with his kidneys, your mother tells you, shaking her head. She has forgotten the name of the illness. A man named Mr. Howard has asked your mother to marry him. He has black hair, black sideburns, black-rimmed glasses. At church picnics, he's always the one who flips hamburgers on the grill. Your mother has said she will let him know.

Your mother is still young and pretty. She spends lots of time at her mirror, putting on green eyeshadow, then creaming it off and putting on blue. Lots of eyeliner, making her eyes look startled and secretive. A tight skirt in a leopard pattern. A pink shiny blouse. Little white plastic boots.

"Wait on the porch," she says, and you go outside where last week's jack-o'-lantern squats discarded on the steps, its grin puckered miserably. Your house backs up to the woods, with its long driveway leading down to Mountain Road. You can hear a pack of beagles running wild in the woods; it disturbs you, that sound of dogs hunting another creature down. You've been afraid of dogs ever since you can remember. It's warm out, but last week was cool enough to redden the leaves of the sweet gum trees.

Your mother comes outside: taptap go her little boots. Part of her hair is pulled up on her head in a braided crown, the rest hangs loose. Her lipstick makes her lips pale.

"Pick some flowers for me, honey," she says, hoisting the jack-o'-lantern in her arms. "Ugh, it's mushy." Together you walk around to the vegetable garden, gone to seed now, the cornstalks broken, the snap vines dried out and tangled like electrical wires. A few portulacas bloom along the last furrow, and some coral chrysanthemums. Your mother heaves the pumpkin into the air. It crashes into the cornstalks, its smile settling against the earth.

You and your mother set out down the long driveway and down Mountain Road. Of course there is no sidewalk, just the soft shoulder of the ground. She's wearing a bell on one boot, and it tinkles. A cricket leaps out of the way. You sniff the chrysanthemums in your hand and sneeze, then pluck some Queen Anne's lace from the roadside and add it to the bouquet.

"Can I get a popsicle at the store?" you ask.

"After we visit Lila."

"Why are we going to see her?"

"Just give her the flowers when she opens the door."

A train is passing when you reach the tracks, and your mother takes your hand and makes you stand far back. Her hair blows around her face. You stare at the wheels, which move so fast they seem to spin backward. Beside the track sits an abandoned freight car, rusty brown, with RF&P in broken white letters. Aren't they ever coming back for it? A redwing blackbird swoops over it.

The man in the caboose waves hard to your mother, but she doesn't wave back. Her bell jingles. "I don't understand," she says, "how weeds can grow in between these tracks with the train running over them all the time."

The old hotel looms before you. You've never been inside it before. You and your mother mount the steps, which are still sturdy and wide with no sag in them. A thin yellow cat, her teats showing, dives beneath a ragged sofa on the porch. You want to look for her kittens, but your mother says, "Come on" and pushes the front door open. It's a small door, considering the size of the building, a double door with cheap frosted-glass windows, put in after the originals were vandalized.

Inside is a musty smell like the seams of used furniture. You're aware of a big room with a long counter along one side, but it's too dim to see well. The wooden floors radiate cold, even through your sandals. The stairway is too close to the front door, its banister held up by skewed posts that look like crooked teeth. Gray metal mailboxes hang beside the staircase, and your mother checks the names. The carpet on the steps is worn away to coarse threads. On the landing, a child's crayon drawing is taped to the wall, and you read the name: Earl Mayhew. He's in your class at school. You envy him the glamour of living in an apartment, even though the building is clearly for poor people. You don't think of your mother as poor, even though she has no money at all.

There's Earl, his monkey face leaning over the banister. "Hey," he says. He wears a blue pajama top over his slacks and holds a doughnut in his hand.

Your mother greets him cheerily, but you feel too shy, too ashamed, to speak to him—because he's a boy, because the doughnut in his hand is too intimate, revealing the universal need to eat.

"I like your bell," he says to your mother, then runs back into his apartment. You hear a woman's voice behind his door, and a baby yelping.

"I think only this wing is occupied," your mother says in the firm voice reserved for adults, yet you hear uncertainty. She pauses on the third floor, brushing her hair with her hands. "She's the only one on this floor, I think."

The third floor is startling, with its open, unscreened window, a broken armchair in a corner of the landing, and newspapers stacked and yellow at the folds. Pipes run from the floor up the walls; something looks wrong with the way they enter the stained ceiling. In the cramped hallway, one wall is yellow, but the paint stops midway up. The rest of the hall is papered in an ancient floral pattern. In the hallway, things lie scattered: a child's torn plastic suitcase, a shadeless lamp that reminds you of a bald man, an empty bookcase with shelves askew, a mattress with stuffing exploding from it like suds. And on a corner of the mattress—

"Kittens!" Four mewing creatures crawl over each other in a nest of newspapers, giving off a milky, furry smell. You touch each small head. Their eyes are still shut.

Your mother locates a door and knocks. The door is cracked. Its thick aqua paint makes an alligator pattern on the panels. The knob sits out, broken, and the keyhole is painted across. You are excited by the age of everything, the sense of fragility.

Your mother knocks again. She whispers to you, "I can't remember what her last name is. Have I ever known it?" She looks incredulous. Finally she calls out, "Lila?"

You go to the big open window on the landing. By craning your head, you can see Lila's balcony. She never hangs laundry out. You see bright white pigeon droppings spattered on balconies below you.

"Lila, it's Ellen Day."

The doorknob rattles from the inside, and your mother shoots you a wild look. The door opens, and there she is—a tiny woman, fierce, gazing up at you, her shoulders no wider than the span of your hands, her skin spotted with brown, her dress something silvery covered with a plaid afghan clutched to her chest. She wears bedroom slippers of a kind sold across the street at the grocery store. Hers are pink. You have the same kind, only green. She wears no socks.

Your mother reaches around and grasps your shoulder, pushing you forward. You lift the flowers to Lila. Her fingers brush yours. They are rough and feline, the pads of a cat's paws.

"May we come in?" asks your mother.

Lila steps back from the door, and you and your mother enter. The room is bigger than you expected, and sunny. Cracks in the walls have been badly spackled. One crack resembles the outline of Virginia. There is a strange little light fixture on the ceiling, its metal base clumsily painted over. At the window hang jacquard curtains so old you can't stop staring at them; then you remember to take in all you can, so you look around at the furniture—a four-poster bed, neatly made, a dresser with a mirror. A mousetrap sits by the baseboard. A table covered with oilcloth holds a box of Ritz crackers, a used teabag in a glass, a box of sugar, a coffee cup with a mismatched saucer, an electric hotplate.

A sink clings to the wall, its pipes covered with blistered white paint. Where would the toilet be? With a child's avidity, your eyes dart to an adjoining chamber, but that door is closed. What about an icebox? How does she keep her food? At a hundred, are crackers and tea enough?

Your mother seems to regret the bell on her shoe and puts one foot on top of the other to quiet it. Lila's eyes meet yours for an instant. She doesn't wear spectacles, as other old ladies do, but her eyes are filmy, like the isinglass on Christmas cards. Your mind races with arithmetic. She was old even when you were born. She will die before you die. You know it and she knows it. The pink slippers move. She lays the flowers on her table.

"I need to ask you about a situation," your mother says, laughing a little. She places her hand on a heart-backed chair but doesn't sit, as Lila hasn't asked her to. "I've wanted to come by anyway, to see how you're getting along."

A pigeon on the balcony casts a huge, grotesque shadow on the wall. The light is lovely—autumn light—and the room is pleasantly warm.

"My husband passed away two years ago. You remember him—Harry Day? And now I have a chance to marry again. Ed Howard. You may know him."

Lila fixes your mother with a gaze. Your mother blanches. You stand close beside her. Bravely she goes on. "I thought you could tell me what you think. If you know anything about him, if I should marry him. Please," and her voice is strained, "should I say yes or no?"

Lila steps nearer. You wonder what she was doing as you and your mother climbed the stairs—just standing in the middle of the floor, waiting?

Her old hand reaches out . . . touches you. Your hair, your cheek. Reaches past your mother to touch you.

"You're the one I helped," she says, her voice so low you wonder if you imagine it. "Your mother was in the store, you were outside. A pack of wild dogs came down the road, sur- rounded you . . ." Her ancient bright face is paler than the white walls. You can't speak, though your brain is doing fire- crackers of recollection: dogs coming nearer, menacing, their breath hot and their eyes savage.

"What do you mean?" cries your mother.

"She was tiny, and the dogs would have eaten her up," Lila says, her voice crackly as if being coaxed off an old waxy record.

Open-mouthed, your mother stares at you. You can neither explain nor confirm, because the memory is just beginning to stir within you at Lila's words. Your mother shakes her head violently.

"Please, what about Ed Howard?" she says.

"Ed Howard," says Lila. "I don't know any Ed Howard. You've come asking me . . ." She smiles. "Good-bye." Her lips close, and you realize too late that you've forgotten to check her teeth. Your mother's bell clinks. Her eyeshadow is messy now. She takes your hand and you move blindly out of the room and down the stairs. Earl Mayhew is waiting at the front door with a stick in his hand. "Want to dig for ants?" he says.

"Go on," you snap at him and instantly regret your anger. He goes out under an oak and twirls the stick into the dirt.

It's colder now. Across the road, the grocery store's lights are cheerful, with a bread truck unloading.

Your mother says, "What was she thinking about? Dogs eating you up? I've always kept my eye on you."

"I don't know," you say, because Lila's words are part of a mystery that lives just beyond your reach, and because you know your mother's scrutiny to be faulty. You seem to recall the dogs' cries, yip-yapping up Mountain Road one dusty day, a wild pack come from the woods, and you were alone on the road except for someone old, someone fearless, driving the dogs away . . . Is it memory or just a story Lila has started for you?

You follow your mother down Mountain Road. Rising wind sweeps the leaves along. The bread truck pulls alongside your mother. The man at the wheel speaks to her.

"Thanks, but we'll walk," your mother says, and the truck drives slowly off.

Mr. Howard is waiting on the porch, smoking, when you get home. He stands up and waves. He's brought a bag of pears, sweet-smelling and golden, bruised with brown.

"Go on in," your mother tells you.

She and Mr. Howard stay outside on the porch. You can't hear what they say, but after a while, Mr. Howard drives away rough and fast, not slow like the bread truck did. You hear dogs barking in the woods again, chuffing up a trail. You're not afraid anymore. Your mother sings in the kitchen: "And in her hair, she wore a yellow ribbon, she wore it for her lover who was far, far away."

You try to remember. You try your best.

The Biggest and the Best

ERIC WARING'S FATHER, Jody, bought the roller rink on a Friday night in May. With the real estate agent, they sat in their station wagon in the deserted parking lot, waiting for the seller. Pollen from a nearby oak tree swept through the windows and made Eric sneeze. He'd brought homework with him, but he couldn't concentrate on the assignment, a chapter on Visigoths.

The building and parking lot had a weedy, abandoned aspect. Eric made out the words "Skate for Fun and Health" in metal script over the door. Every time he looked up from his history book, his eyes met those of the realtor, reflected in the side mirror of the car. Somehow he felt nervous around her.

"I hope this guy hurries up," said the realtor, whose name was Clarkie Tabb. She checked her wristwatch. "I'm on my way to a twins' convention in Washington, DC."

Eric's father asked, "Does your twin look like you?"

"There was some resemblance, but she's dead. She died when we were five years old," said Clarkie, balancing her briefcase on her lap and unsnapping it. She took out a packet of prunes and nibbled them. The licorice-like scent drifted to the back seat. Eric tried to picture Clarkie Tabb with a twin sister. Clarkie went on, "Once a twin, always a twin. Sometimes I wonder if I was the one who died and she's the one still alive. If our mother got us mixed up, I mean." She shrugged. "Anyway, I've lived so long without her."

Eric's father took a flat, clear bottle from his pocket and sipped from it. Clarkie turned toward him. She had the biggest face Eric had ever seen; even in profile it was large. She said to Eric's father, "Once this purchase is all settled, Jody, I'm counting on you to give me a ride to the train station."

"But you don't have any suitcases," Eric's father said, and hiccupped.

Clarkie laughed. From the briefcase she lifted a toothbrush and a fistful of gleaming, satiny garments. "I've got everything I need."

Eric leaned forward and asked her, "What was your twin's name?"

Clarkie stuffed the shiny clothes away and said over her shoulder, "Her name was Alma." She paused and then said, "I bet you wish I'd shut up so you could get your homework done. You're in seventh grade, right? Have you taken algebra? That's what I call fun."

Usually Eric liked people who liked math, but he pictured Clarkie lecturing the vanished Alma about equations, and the image troubled him. He felt oddly sad about this long-ago child.

Behind them, a horn honked.

Eric's father said, "I believe Mr. Pinchefsky has arrived." He took another pull from the bottle and got out of the car. Eric was sharply conscious of being alone with Clarkie. Echoes of his father's voice reached him, as if from underwater. He watched his father shaking hands with a burly man in a horizontally striped shirt. The man looked like a giant bee.

Before Eric knew he was going to say anything, a question popped out of his mouth. "How did Alma die?"

Clarkie turned to him avidly, her blue eyes black in the dimness of the car, her nails digging into the headrest of her seat. "All right, I'll tell you how she died, if you tell me something. Deal? Does your father really want to divorce your mother?"

Eric felt sick. "What does that have to do with anything?" His father and the striped man were strolling toward the roller rink, their shapes blurred in the dusk. When he looked back at Clarkie, her eyes held his, hard. She reached back to the book on his lap and clapped it shut.

"If they divorce," she said, "I get to handle the sale of your house. At first, Jody was real eager to move ahead with things. But now, well, I can't tell who's slowing all this down, him or your mother or their lawyers."

Eric's father waved and called, "Come on, Clarkie, Eric. Mr. Pinchefsky's in a hurry."

"I'm coming," said Clarkie. To Eric she said, "So tell me. Do they want a divorce or don't they?"

"Did you kill Alma?" he said.

Clarkie's big face blanched, her lips going white within an outline of red. "You don't deserve to know what happened to her." She got out of the car and slammed the door.

After a moment, Eric followed her. The air was the color of shadows. He stood behind his father as the adults passed a clipboard and papers around, their hair fluttering in the gritty breeze. Mr. Pinchefsky said to Eric, "You'll have a powerful lot of good times now that your daddy owns this place." He grinned, but he looked unhappy.

Eric nodded. He'd never been inside the rink. It had been closed ever since he could remember. He couldn't wait to go in.

Jody signed the papers with his big loopy writing and handed Mr. Pinchefsky a check. "I'm still not sure why you're selling," he said, "but hey, don't change your mind. This place is a great investment, the biggest and best roller rink in all of Virginia. I remember when people used to come here from all over."

"Well, you know I haven't actually operated it in a while," said Mr. Pinchefsky. He handed a key to Jody. "It has a few cobwebs. Needs sprucing up."

"I bet you can still do a mean figure eight," Clarkie said to Mr. Pinchefsky.

"I want to spend more time with my cats," he said, "and my ham radio. Last night I picked up somebody in Saskatchewan."

"That's enigmatic of you," said Jody.

Eric pictured Mr. Pinchefsky skating, a big unsteady bee shorn of its wings, surrounded by a buzzing swarm of other skaters.

Jody offered Mr. Pinchefsky the flat bottle, but he waved it away. Clarkie did too, saying, "I never drink before I travel."

Eric's school was just down the road. The sounds of an evening softball game floated to his ears, and he wished he were there, with a bag of popcorn in his hands, cheering the junior varsity team with his friends.

Jody took a big swallow from the bottle. "Rhymes with rink," he said.

As Mr. Pinchefsky drove off, Eric said, "Can we go inside, Dad?"

"Sure," Jody said.

"We don't have time," said Clarkie. "My train."

"What the hell kind of cats does he have, anyway?" Jody said. "Tigers?" He laughed and drank some more.

Clarkie said, "Jody, why don't you come to Washington with me? You need a vacation."

"You need a drink," he said.

"I dare you to go," she said.

"You're not a twin, Dad," Eric said, but his father was smiling at Clarkie.

"We can be back by Sunday night," Clarkie said. "You're allowed five minutes to stop by your place to pack."

Jody tossed Eric the key to the roller rink. "I'll drop you at your mother's," he said.

"But Dad!" said Eric.

"The biggest and best roller rink in the whole state of Virginia," Clarkie said, easing into the car. She slid over to the driver's seat and buckled herself in.

Eric and his father stood outside the car. Eric said, "Dad, don't you miss Mom?"

His father closed his eyes, spread out his arms, and swayed as if the warm evening breeze would carry him away. "My grief is a guttering candle," he said. He straightened and looked toward the woman behind the windshield. "I guess it's too late to bribe Mr. Pinchefsky to go in my place," he said, and chuckled.

When they were all in the car, Eric's father fell asleep. Clarkie drove fast down Jamestown Road to Eric's house, where, until a few months ago, Eric's father had lived with Eric and his mother. Parking the car across the street from the house, Clarkie turned her big face back to Eric. He expected her to say good night, but she didn't say anything. He gathered his books and got out of the car.

He waited in the driveway until they drove off. It was fully dark, with flashes of heat lightning in the sky. An image came to him of little Alma, the twin, in a bathtub. A five-year-old version of Clarkie threw something at her—a radio or a hair dryer. It landed in the water, hissing and sparking, and Alma was electrocuted.

The windows of his house were dark. He had seen no reason to tell his father that his mother was away for the weekend herself, at a tournament with a golf pro she was dating. The golfer was a tall, sleepy-looking man who had never been inside the house. When he visited Eric's mother, he would always sit on the front porch swing, "to protect your dignity," he told her, while she smiled. But they had progressed suddenly from the front porch to a tournament in South Carolina. Eric's mother had instructed Eric to spend the weekend with his father, at the apartment Jody had rented since the separation.

Eric unlocked the door and went inside. The familiar living room was more orderly now that his father had moved out, taking with him his overflowing desk and leaving calm spaces which his mother had filled with potted plants and bowls of potpourri. How quiet it was. Eric went to his mother's piano and drew his fingers down the ivories in a long ripple, low to high.

IT FELT odd to wake up on a Saturday and realize first that he was alone in the house, and second, that he had plans to go to school. There was to be a special program in the gym, something so ballyhooed you had to pay to get in—a performance by someone called the Amazing Trick Basketball Shooter. Eric pulled on his clothes, ate a bowl of ice cream, and headed to school.

He couldn't find his friends, so he sat in the first empty space he found in the crowded bleachers. The principal, Mr. Moore, stood up and gave an important-sounding introduction for the guest, whose name was Wilfred Beachy and who had given shows all over the country. Eric leaned forward.

The Amazing Trick Basketball Shooter strutted to the center of the shiny floor, rolling a basketball on his back, from shoulder to shoulder. When the applause quieted, he aimed at the hoop from near and far, twisting his body and tossing the ball from odd angles.

Eric was taken aback. Not only was Wilfred Beachy ancient, with bandaged knees and flailing arms, but he missed all his shots. Giggles rose from the bleachers and gave way to guffaws. Again and again, the ball bounced off the rim or didn't even get close.

Hecklers booed and made rude sounds. Wilfred Beachy scooped the ball from its wretched stillness on the floor, then layupped with his legs going limp as a doll's. He tried an upside-down-between-the-knees shot. He butted the ball toward the hoop with his head. He spun and hurled the ball from mid-spin. He failed every time, the loose white gristle of his arms and thighs sagging. Once he was close enough to the bleachers that Eric could see age spots on his scalp, under his thin gray hair, and hear his hot gasps. The whites of his eyes were a yolky yellow. He looked like he belonged in a hospital. Eric could tell he was really trying, not missing on purpose.

The crowd's mirth soared higher. Sometimes Eric laughed too, helplessly, though he felt bad about it. Mr. Moore stared balefully at the trick shooter, then strode out the double doors of the gym. The doors swung behind him, their glass panes, reinforced with chicken wire, framing his retreating figure.

The Amazing Trick Shooter tried a hook shot and missed. "Talk about a fraud," said a girl sitting behind Eric.

The sound of heckling rose to a high gabble.

"Quiet, everybody!" yelled Ms. Fritter, a hockey coach. She rose from her seat and said, "Y'all are ruining his concentration." She sat down again.

Wilfred Beachy flubbed an easy shot from the foul line. "And the stands went wild," the girl behind Eric said. "This is pathetic."

Eric turned around and said, "Shut up." He saw that he had just rebuked the homecoming princess. Her long black hair fell in a curtain around her beautiful face. Nobody ever contradicted her. She frowned, as if uncertain about what she had heard. Eric turned around in his seat and felt her eyes burning the back of his neck.

"The only thing amazing about this guy is that he defies the odds," a logical-sounding boy behind Eric said to the homecoming princess. "You'd think, statistically speaking, he could get a few on the basis of luck."

The crowd's laughter hummed at an even level, like cicadas on a summer night. Eric wondered how the old man stood it—not just failure, but mockery.

"This is very boring," the princess said. "I might demand my money back."

The logical-voiced boy said, "Why doesn't he just retire? Go home, wherever that is. He must be a hundred years old."

"Absolutely," said the princess. "This was funny at first, but now . . ." She sighed. "I have too much to do to be here, watching this idiot."

Eric turned around and faced her. Her eyes, almond-shaped and long-lashed, met his with liquid hostility. Her beauty was an arrow in his heart, but he said, "Someday I'm going to be rich. I'll have a pool and I'll give all these great parties, and you won't ever be invited."

The princess gasped. The Amazing Trick Shooter concluded with a spate of dribbling as loud and fast as gunfire, and everybody flung themselves off the bleachers and out of the gym.

OUTSIDE THE school, the logical-voiced boy wanted to fight, but Eric ran away, feeling cowardly and hunted. He headed for the woods behind the school and jumped an oozy creek. Then he remembered the key in his pocket.

Catching his breath, he took shortcuts until he reached the roller rink. In daylight, it looked bleak, marked with old graffiti. He stood on the same spot where the previous night his father and Clarkie had decided to go to Washington. The oak pollen was as bad as ever, stinging his nose.

Behind him, a sharp voice rang out. "Hey. Where can I get a corn dog?" A giant blue car pulled up beside him, with the Amazing Trick Shooter leaning out the window.

Eric regarded him. The man did not appear humble, considering that he had just been publicly humiliated. He looked older than ever, and mad.

"Are you deaf?" he said. "I said a corn dog. Were you at my show just now?"

Eric nodded.

The old man lifted his hands off the steering wheel and flopped them back and forth. "My wrists hurt," he said. "I give my all. Fair food, that's what keeps me going. Barbecue, roast corn, tacos. I got my own cotton candy machine at home."

Eric didn't know where to get a corn dog. The only restaurants he could think of were fast food places or fancy ones that served colonial-type food. "Where's home?" he asked.

"The Missouri bootheel," came the answer, importantly. Then the old man pointed at the roller rink in a gesture of discovery and said, "Look. I bet they've got corn dogs. Roller rinks have some of the best food. Ain't it open? No cars around."

"It's closed, but it'll reopen soon," Eric said. "I own it. Well, my dad does. He bought it last night. I think my mother owns it, too, half of it." He hadn't thought of this before, and he wondered if Jody and Clarkie had considered it. His parents were still married. Or were they?

"Maybe there's food in there anyway," the old man said. The blue car trembled, as if ready to leap forward.

"Any food in there is probably real old," Eric said.

The trick shooter grunted. "If you're too cheap to give a traveling man a meal, then let me use your phone. This is a town that I've got kin in."

Eric spied a rusty pay phone outside the rink and said, "You can use that one."

The trick shooter drove toward it, with Eric trotting beside him. The old man asked, "So what did you think of my performance?"

Eric hesitated. "You missed a lot."

"That's not the point. What I do is art. It's beauty." He pulled up beside the phone and got out of the car, holding a tattered address book. Still wearing his frayed undershirt and shorts, he smelled sweaty, and his chest heaved. "Got any change?"

Eric gave him a quarter. "Who are you going to call?"

"Oh, my niece." The old man fumbled through the address book. "Little gal's a real estate agent now, making herself one tidy pile of dough."

"Clarkie!" Eric said. "Do you mean Clarkie Tabb?"

"You know her? I keep thinking she's about your age. I can't picture her grown up. Last I saw her, she was so teensy, she fell into my cotton candy machine. Got cotton candy stuck all over her. Her mother had to cut her hair off and shave her eyebrows." He cackled, plunking the quarter into the phone.

Excitement swept over Eric. "What happened to Alma? Clarkie's twin?"

The yellow eyes flew open wide. "How do you know about Alma? That was a terrible thing, just awful." He dialed, squinting at his address book.

"She's not home," Eric said. "She's at a twins' convention in Washington, DC. What did happen to Alma? Did Clarkie do something bad to her?"

The old man dropped the phone. The receiver dangled, buzzing, from its cord. He ducked into his car, brought out his basketball, and tossed it to Eric. Eric caught it. It felt hard as a cannonball. Wilfred Beachy said, "Lemme give you the best advice you'll ever get. When you throw that ball, throw it like it's somebody you love but are sick of. Put it here!" He raised his arms, and Eric lobbed it to him. Wilfred smacked the ball lightly into his car. He tore a sheet of paper from his address book and wrote on it. "My autograph."

Eric took the paper. The signature was illegible.

"I ought to hit the road," said Wilfred Beachy. "Got a show in Roanoke tonight."

"Want to skate?" Eric said. "Want to see if there's food?"

"Why not?" said Wilfred Beachy.

Eric took the key from his pocket and unlocked the door. How dark it was inside. Dust motes swirled in the beam of sunshine cast by the open door. He found a light switch that worked, and surveyed the giant room: a musty arena of polished wood, a snack bar with "Pizza Nachos Root Beer" chalked on a blackboard, and a wall of shelves that held skates in all sizes, giving off a leathery, feety smell. He hadn't roller-skated since he was little, and then he'd worn the metal kind of skates that you attached to your shoes. These were serious skates.

At the snack bar, they found cans of grape soda, a bag of pebble-hard marshmallows, and a box of animal crackers. Wilfred Beachy fell on the food, smacking his lips as he ate.

Eric went to the shelves of skates, chose a brown, bump-toed pair, and rolled the wheels against his palm. The leather around the ankles was stretched, which was reassuring, as if the previous wearers had found them comfortable. He took off his shoes, pulled on the skates, tied the worn laces, and clumped into the rink. The handrail was tempting, but he didn't want to look like a sissy. He scraped his feet backward and forward. A rough unvarnished patch caught him and he fell, his butt slamming to the floor, his legs weighted with the skates.

Wilfred Beachy gave a deep snort. Eric picked himself up and kept going. The rhythm of his legs took over, and within minutes he achieved a smooth rapid glide. The walls whipped by as he flew faster, faster, the rink all his own.

Above him, a big sign was flashing. GRAND MARCH. Eric stopped and stared.

"I found the lights," Wilfred Beachy called. "Look at this." He fiddled with some controls behind the snack bar, and the sign changed, lighting up with the words ALL SKATE.

Eric was delighted. "Come on," he said. "Grab some skates." Suddenly, he felt great. He knew what he wanted to do—operate the roller rink and make it successful. His parents, thrilled, would get back together. He pictured them waltzing around the rink on silver wheels.

Wilfred Beachy flipped another lever, and music boomed out from hidden speakers—a symphony of violins, trumpets, and cymbals. A mirrored ball on the ceiling was revolving, glittering, turning red, purple, pink, and green. Staring at it, Eric fell again.

Wilfred Beachy zoomed past him, hooting, his arms held wide. "Watch!" he cried.

Wilfred's breeze fanned Eric's face. The old man circled away, and Eric dizzily got to his feet. Evidently Wilfred Beachy knew the music. Dipping and swaying to the tickling violins and roguish oboes, he bent his knees and rolled low and tight, then burst forward in a leap that took his skates clear off the floor. The music changed to a rumba, and Wilfred swerved backwards, trailing a high, wild chuckle, his eyes closed.

"Look out!" Eric said.

Wilfred Beachy crashed into the wall, shuddered, and lay sprawled beneath the rail, his wheels spinning, catching the purple and chartreuse light. He lay very still.

Eric cried out and skated to him, knocking into Wilfred's shin. The pungent odor of hours-old sweat steamed to Eric's nostrils. Eric put his hand on the thin undershirt and felt Wilfred's heart going hard and fast.

Wilfred stirred and said, "I'd almost forgotten about Alma. Now I can see her plain as day, such a fine, sweet child." He struggled to sit up.

For a moment, the little girl's presence hovered beside them, as if she too were skating and had paused, out of breath, to help her uncle.

"Can you stand up?" Eric asked. "Want me to call an ambulance?"

"Just help me up," Wilfred said, and Eric hauled him to his feet. Wilfred said, "I'm all right. I'm fine. Thanks for lunch." He kicked off his skates, found his old sneakers, and wobbled toward the door. Eric took off his skates and hurried to follow him outside.

Wilfred tucked himself into his car and roared off. Exhaust left a rubbery reek in the air. Eric stood in the parking lot while the blue car disappeared. Roanoke was hours away, far enough that when darkness came, Wilfred would still be on the road.

Did Clarkie feel this alone after Alma died? Eric thought of how the roller rink had been closed his whole life, and of all the years that added up to, years when Wilfred Beachy was driving around giving shows. He surveyed the broken blacktop of the parking lot. He didn't believe it would ever fill with people slamming car doors and calling out to each other. It was hard to imagine it had ever been as busy and prosperous a place as his father had claimed. That was during some vanished time, years ago, when his father was a boy and when even Wilfred Beachy was young. Yet he felt a surge of loyalty for the place.

He went back inside and put both pairs of skates back on the shelf among the dozens of other pairs, aware of the hundreds of unknown hands that had tied the laces. A few skates contained rumpled socks. Except for himself and Wilfred, all the skaters, whoever they might be, were now years older than when they'd worn the skates. Some of them were people who still lived around here, kids who had grown up, or grownups who were now middle-aged or old. There would have been families, people on dates, and groups of kids, or people just by themselves. Some of them must have moved away, and some of them were gone forever.

As he walked home, his legs still held the razzmatazz motion of the skates; his knees were suction cups of wind. His house was as empty and still as before. Afternoon sunshine turned the dust on the furniture gold. He had never heard such quiet before, the quiet of his own house.

The phone rang. He could do like grownups sometimes did, and not answer. His father did that a lot, and sometimes his mother, too, but he reached for it.

His father said, "That woman picked a fight with me and threw my clothes away. Then she gave me this stupid T-shirt. I'm at the train station in DC. Is your mother there?"

"She's out somewhere," Eric said. He pictured her hoisting a flag on a golf green so her boyfriend could make a putt.

There was noise in the background, and Eric strained to hear his father. Jody said, "So I have on this idiotic shirt Clarkie gave me. It says, Beep Beep I Won a Jeep. She really did. Are you okay?"

"I went skating," Eric said. "You bought a great place."

"Gee, I'd almost forgotten about that," his father said. "I'll be back tonight."

"Dad," Eric said. "Did Clarkie say anymore about her twin? You know, Alma?"

"The very name Clarkie is poison. Don't utter it. Hey, my train's boarding."

"Are you and Mom getting back together?" Eric said.

"I better go."

Eric wanted to say that he no longer cared how Alma had died. He had pried into her short life too much already, and he was just sorry she was gone. But his father said so long and hung up the phone.

Heaven

TOWARD THE END of 1918, with so many sick from flu, Margaret Taylor stopped receiving visitors who wanted to consult her prophesying horse; she was afraid they would bring the plague. The horse, Lady Wisdom, who spelled out answers by plunking her hooves on the wooden blocks of a large typewriter-like contraption, spent her time resting in the barn or grazing in the pasture. Lady Wisdom knew the epidemic would pass, that she and Margaret and Margaret's son Barlow would live, and that customers would come again in the spring.

Sometimes, of course, Lady Wisdom was wrong: she had jumped the gun on Armistice Day and predicted war's end two weeks early.

"You're an optimist," said Margaret to the horse, hugging her neck, flipping the ragged mane with her fingers.

Optimist and golden goose—Lady Wisdom brought in money, not a fortune, but enough. At three questions for a dollar, who could resist asking, *Who will I marry? Where can I find my lost watch? Will I ever get rich? Will I get a crop this year? What should I do?*

People came out to the Taylors' Henrico County farm from Richmond, Ashland, Petersburg, and Fredericksburg. They came from as far away as James City County to the east and Charlottesville to the west. Lady Wisdom warned them of false lovers, of storms that could ruin their fields. Many asked, "Will my son come home from the war?"

Some were told no, and then Barlow and his mother had to lead them from the barn, help them stumble back to their cars, while they screamed and wept, saying, "Your horse is a liar. I'll get the police on you. My boy's coming home. I just had a letter from him."

"How would you feel if that horse said *he* was gonna die?" demanded a freckle-faced woman, pointing at Barlow.

"We'll all die, someday," Barlow's mother said.

"So will your fool horse," the woman said, a woman for whom Lady Wisdom had just spelled out "Argonne Forest" on her wooden machine. "Your horse'll die too," the woman said.

"She knows it," said Margaret Taylor.

Lady Wisdom had been asked many times to predict the date of her own death. She would plunk out the answer on her machine as if it were any other date. Barlow hated the people who asked that question, just as he grieved for the ones who were told their soldier sons would die.

So the flu time was almost a relief, a respite. Visitors' lost brooches malingered in small dark places. People who drove out to the Taylors' farm were sent away.

"Tell me what it's like," Miss Foyt said, keeping him after school while they cleaned the room together. "Do you love the horse?"

"Yes," said Barlow.

"Are you afraid of her, the way she knows things?"

When he didn't answer, she said gently, "That's all right. You can love somebody and be afraid of them too. The paper said your father bought her for a plow horse and then your mother realized she was special. Is that how it was? The paper said your mother used to count the rows she had plowed, and the horse would stamp her feet that many times, and then your mother knew. And that was years ago," Miss Foyt went on, "before you were born."

"Yes," said Barlow. He had often seen reporters interviewing his mother. She was patient with them.

Miss Foyt set down her bucket and wiped her shining cheeks. With her cascade of soft hair and her high voice, she was beautiful; how could he not love her? She stood in front of him to ask, "Could you do something for me, Barlow?"

"What?"

"Ask Lady Wisdom if Mr. Graham will ever marry me. It's been so long."

"It don't work that way," Barlow said. "You have to ask her yourself. Or at least be there, with Ma asking her. Ma says it's hard work."

"Is it the horse or your mother that has this ability?" she said.

"Both of 'em together," said Barlow.

"The things your mother must know," said Miss Foyt.

"She don't gossip," he protested, for he had heard her reassure people, time and again.

"She don't?" Miss Foyt asked, smiling. "Doesn't, Barlow." She paused. "Don't tell anybody what I said about Mr. Graham."

"I won't," he said.

"Do you ask Lady Wisdom for the answers to your lessons?" He shook his head.

She said, "I would ask her about everything. I'd stay up all night, asking her questions. I'll never understand how she does what she does, but it's wonderful. You must have great restraint, Barlow."

"Thank you, ma'am."

"Are they magic, Barlow? The horse? Your mother?"

"I don't know," he said.

"I'm so tired! Here, let's put this old bucket away and go home," she said. "It's already dark out."

"I'll walk you home," he said.

She smiled. "Ten years old, and walking me home. No, dear, you go on." She rubbed her temple. "Oh, my head hurts."

She didn't come to school the next day. The day after that, she was dead of flu and buried.

A HEAVY snow fell. Barlow's mother said, "This will kill the flu."

But Miss Foyt was dead and buried. Barlow cried as he gave Lady Wisdom her hay and water in the barn. Snow swirled beneath the door and stuck to his shoes.

When he went back to the house, he found a man there, talking to his mother, a man with a black mustache.

"How much," the man said.

"She's not for sale," his mother said.

"You could live better," the man said. "Send the boy to a fine school. Your farm isn't worth much."

"She's not for sale."

"She could die. She could be stolen or shot," the man said. "You'd have nothing then."

"Get out of here," said Barlow, from the doorway. He had never said those words to anybody before.

The man laughed, his teeth strong and yellow beneath the mustache.

"It's all right, Barlow," his mother said. "I've invited him for supper."

Later, Barlow heard them in his mother's room. He imagined his mother's clothes on a chair—the brown dress and pearls she always wore, pretty fake pearls, unless she was out in the fields. Then she wore her overalls.

In the morning, the man was gone. The snow was gone, too, and the air was balmy out, with a booming wind. Barlow smelled wild onions in Lady Wisdom's pasture.

"My mother saved her pee during the old war," his mother said, "the war between the states. People saved it for the niter in it, to use in gunpowder."

Already he missed the war, and it had only been over a few days. He knew he shouldn't. But he had saved, too, had saved dried peach pits and put them in a box which Miss Foyt had sent away. The pits were used in gas masks, somehow. Miss Foyt had explained it. She had said they were all helping, so very much.

His mother was counting their money. What she didn't keep in the bank, she kept in a green glass vase. She said, "Yes, Mama saved her pee, and they used bark for shoe soles and thorns for hypodermic needles. That's how they inoculated themselves against smallpox, back then. And young girls braided beautiful jewelry out of dead people's hair."

His mother drew him close. Her hands smelled like the money, and her pearls pressed into his cheek. "There," she said. "Rest your head on my shoulder. I know you loved her."

HE HAD thought Lady Wisdom would spell out "heaven." But she just stood there, her great eyes blazing, her leathery coat steaming, her mane twitching, her hoof-sized wooden keys silent before her.

"And Daddy?" he said. "Where is he?"

Each letter crashed like an earthquake as she stomped out, *Gone.*

But he already knew that. His father had fallen off a ladder while picking cherries, right out in the backyard.

"Fell down like a sack, dead," his mother always said. "It wasn't the fall that killed him. He had a heart attack. You were only a few months old. He built the writing machine for Lady Wisdom just weeks before he died."

"We were happy together," she always said.

SMITH DAM, Lady Wisdom spelled out for the benefit of two policemen who came all the way from Roanoke. Barlow's mother rubbed the horse's neck and murmured to her as she always did.

"That's all she can tell you," she told the men.

"The dam on Smith Mountain Lake? We searched there already," one policeman—the chief—said impatiently, scratching at a sore place on his cheek. "Those kids aren't there," he said. "Ask her again."

Barlow's mother sighed. Barlow thought she looked tired. He spoke up: "She'd tell you if there was more."

The policemen glared at him. The one who kept scratching his face said, "Son, there's two children missing, about your age. Don't you want them found? Think how their folks must feel."

"Yoo-hoo!" a voice called. A young woman on a bicycle rolled up to the barn door, panting for breath. "I have a question for the horse," she said. "Where do I pay?"

"We're closed," Barlow said.

"But it's important," the woman said. "I rode all the way out here."

"I'm sorry," Barlow's mother said.

"But they're here," the woman said, indicating the policemen. She said quickly, "What's wrong? What happened?"

"Ma'am, we have to ask you to leave," said the police chief.

The woman stared at the men, the horse, and Barlow's mother, who stood beside Lady Wisdom with her hand on the bridle. The woman opened her mouth to speak, then turned and pedaled away, her dress flying up behind her.

"I'm sure that sort of interference doesn't help, Mrs. Taylor," the younger policeman said kindly.

"If you could just ask her one more time," the chief said.

Damn, Lady Wisdom spelled out.

Barlow burst out laughing and ran from the barn. Way down the road, the lady on the bicycle was a bouncing speck.

They learned from the paper that the children were found after all: a brother and sister in faraway Franklin County, their bodies trapped in the rocks below the dam on Smith Mountain Lake. They had been fishing when the water rose and drowned them. Their broken rods, a trout still caught on a hook, were wrapped around them.

The paper did not mention Lady Wisdom.

"They hate to use us," Barlow's mother told him, "but they'll be back. I don't mind. I never do."

She was frying apples at the stove. Apples and sausage, his favorite. "Why don't you ask why?" she said. "Why other animals can't?"

"You told me already that Lady Wisdom's special," he said, thinking: the counting, the plowed rows. But you know the answers too. Why don't I?

"Eat," she said, filling his plate.

AT CHRISTMASTIME, the man with the mustache took them to the circus. In a pavilion draped with cedar boughs, he bought them sauerkraut, blood pudding, cider, and peanuts. He held Barlow's mother tightly around her waist. Clowns with sloppy buckets of water tried to put out a fire in a cardboard house but only made it worse. A fierce man in a loincloth made white tigers leap and cower, and a bear danced on its hind legs, twirling a parasol. Barlow's mother laughed and clapped her hands. Barlow blew on his cup of hot cider but burned his tongue anyway.

"I'll show you the good stuff," the man said and took them to a row of tents. He paid and took them inside.

Pinheads and dwarves were there, giants and bearded ladies, each in a booth or on a stage. The dim air smelled of incense. *Half-man, half-woman,* a sign said, and a shadow hovered behind a pale curtain.

"Baboon child," a barker hollered, pointing to a cage.

Barlow's mother stormed out, the mustached man chasing after her through the crowd, his feet chuffing up sawdust. Barlow stayed.

A big woman with a shawl over her chest waved him near. She was seated on a tall chair, tilting her head as she smoked a cigarette.

"Touch her," she said and drew her shawl away. Barlow saw half of a tiny person growing out of her chest, a partial body protruding from her dress. It was nude, a buttocks and a pair of legs which stirred gently, the skin baby-smooth. He could see a flap of skin where it connected to the woman's body.

"Is it your baby?" he asked.

"She's my twin," she said. "I was born with her. Don't be scared. Touch her. Tickle her feet. I can feel it, myself, whenever she is touched."

Barlow put out his hand. He stroked the pink heels, lifted up his hand and touched the small behind. The little legs pumped as if pushing a swing. The woman closed her eyes and said, "You're touching her now, and now, and now."

"ARE YOU going to marry him?" he asked his mother.

"No," she said. "He's married now. He's so good-looking, yet he took an ugly bride. That's what he told me. He said it felt like sweet poison."

"Why did he marry her?" Barlow said. White tigers sprang through his brain. Cherries spilled from a half-full sack. His feet flipped off the rungs of a ladder.

"It doesn't matter now," she said, humming, fixing her hair a different way. From her dresser, she picked up a seashell and held it to her ear, closing her eyes.

Stolen or shot, and then you'd have nothing. He heard the man's words as he trudged to school in the morning and chopped wood at night. Snow fell again, and this time it stayed, a crusty cover on the ground, slick and blue in the twilight when ice formed.

"You're growing up so fine and strong," his mother told him, gazing over the top of her book as he stoked the fire. "You can do so many things."

TIME HAD told: every mother and father who asked, "Will my son come home from the war?" had an answer now. Still Lady Wisdom rested. When people knocked on the door or clustered around the barn, their footprints forming melted spots in the snow, Barlow went and told them, "We're closed. Come back in the spring."

AT SCHOOL, they were studying Mexico. The new teacher, an impatient young pastor, pointed to a map, where Mexico was colored gold. The people were very poor, he told the class. They rode on donkeys.

Barlow daydreamed about cars. He knew all the kinds and loved them: Oldsmobile, Reo, Stanley, Hupmobile, Packard, Pope-Hartford, Haynes Apperson, Locomobile, Model T.

"—will stay after school and maybe then you'll learn to pay attention," the teacher said, while the other students laughed.

Miss Foyt had handled this bucket, the one he dunked the mop in to wash the floor. The schoolroom was silent except for the clock. The teacher slouched at his desk, staring at the map of Mexico, while Barlow scrubbed. The clock ticked.

The teacher moved his gaze from the map to Barlow and said angrily, "When I was your age, boys threw me on a blanket and tossed me up and down until I vomited. They were Satan's helpers, weren't they?"

Barlow gripped the mop. The man scowled and said, "You can go now."

Barlow got out fast, dumping the water out the back door.

His mother was waiting in front of the barn, a lantern in her hand making a circle of light in the dusk.

"Is Lady Wisdom all right?" he cried—but there was the horse in her pasture, nosing tufts of grass out of the snow.

"She's fine," his mother said. "I was just waiting for you."

She had been crying. She said her lover's name. "He was hurt today," she said. "He fell when he was getting off a streetcar, in the city. Lady Wisdom knows it, too. Look at her ears. He'll be all right, thank God."

"Let's go away," Barlow said. "You and Lady Wisdom and me. Let's go to Mexico."

His mother looked at him steadily, her face very still.

"I mean it," he said.

"Bring her on in," she said, opening the pasture gate.

He led Lady Wisdom into the barn. The horse's eyes snapped like lightning; her foggy breath unfurled into the hay.

His mother said, "I love him, Barlow."

With a shovel, he broke the ice in the trough. It made a glassy darkness, floating in the water. He saw again the circus lady's twin, the pearly little body with the waving legs, and he thought: I wonder if it grew out of her heart.

The Blue Monkey

AFTER MY HUSBAND Ed and I lost our only child, our daughter Cyndy, we were invited to join a supper club. People felt sorry for us. We don't belong in a supper club. That's for lawyers and surgeons, people like that. I didn't want to join, but Ed insisted. The pressures of the supper club are enormous. You have to serve the right wines, plural, with the right flowers and music and china. You have to have the right talk, about travel. My husband Ed, the sheriff, is called a lawman by these people, a title they pronounce archly and which he relishes. They love his stories. They make exceptions to the travel talk, for him.

When it was our turn to host, I served Seafood Newburg made from imitation crab, along with green rice, the kind with chopped parsley and chicken bouillon cubes, and my best dessert, chocolate pudding layered with toasted nuts and Cool Whip. Rosé wine all evening.

Mimsy, a lawyer's wife, took me aside and said, "Why not serve canned spaghetti or tuna sandwiches? Rent a karaoke machine?" Only the curling fury in her voice gave her away. Those Botoxed faces look so reasonable.

"You have to admit it was good," I said. "Next time it'll be oven-fried chicken, coated in instant potato flakes, and a cold salad made with LeSeur peas and Wish-Bone dressing."

Bereavement makes me untouchable. Mimsy said, "Oh, God, you're fixing her favorite foods, aren't you? Your daughter's favorites? I'll clean up, Helen. It's okay."

The kitchen door swung open, and there was my lover, Buddy, turning in his dessert plate and risking a kiss on my cheek. His wife is the best cook in the club. They both teach history at the college and give tours of historic Cedar Mount, their beautiful home.

Buddy said to me, "That was a classic meal. Don't you ever go faddish on us." This was a dig at Mimsy, who cooks Thai. "If you ever serve tapas, Helen, honey, you're out of the club."

"Nobody talks about tapas anymore," said Mimsy. Loading the dishwasher, she gave the impression of dumping bodies into a trench. "Passé. Like Veal Oscar, or endive. Or watermelon with kirsch."

"You've done enough, Mimsy," I said, and eased her and Buddy both out the swinging door.

Buddy said over his shoulder, "Cool Whip tastes as good as crème fraîche. Better." He mouthed, "Tomorrow?" And I nodded.

Anything that wasn't already loaded in the dishwasher, I threw away—wineglasses, salad forks I'd borrowed from Mimsy, and a platter I'd have had to wash by hand. That didn't suit me, a big wasteful gesture. The next morning I fished everything out of the trash and washed and dried it.

What is it like to be married to the sheriff? Used to be, when I heard of a jailbreak, I took a wrapped sandwich and a dollar bill to the end of my driveway and left them on the road. Today an armed robber named Pigram got out of prison in the morning, and by lunchtime Ed had arrested him again. Pigram was at home. Who can blame somebody for just going home? But I don't leave sandwiches and money on the road anymore.

Cyndy would have liked the story of Pigram. She'd have said, "Awww" about Ed's finding him at home. Our daughter, who sculpted in light, whose blue monkey neon sign I see at a popular bar every time I drive to town: when she was a child, she used to walk with me to drop off the sandwich and the dollar bill.

The bar—the Blue Monkey—is shutting down. The manager has agreed to sell me the blue neon monkey that Cyndy made. It's the most valuable thing in the place. Come get it today, the manager said, because tonight, after the last drink is sold, that's it. Otherwise it'll go at auction, along with the glasses, the stools, and the big TV. I'll pay him an extraordinary sum for the blue monkey, but gladly. Cyndy was proud of it.

Somebody always got the sandwiches and the money that Cyndy and I left on the road. *Was it you?* Cyndy and I asked each other, when we checked the next day. *Did you come and take 'em away?*

No, we assured each other. *The man got 'em, the one on the run, and it'll help him, won't it, and maybe he's a good man after all.*

Maybe stray dogs ate the sandwiches (baloney and cheese, Cyndy's favorite) and the wax paper too, and the money blew away. No, never. Always it was somebody hungry and hunted, finding enough to keep him going, thanking us in his heart, a man who had run at a crouch through barbed wire and dodged the shots of the guards, finding in that wax paper the best meal of his life.

Ed is good-looking. He wears a short, graying beard and tinted sunglasses: that look. He listens to recordings of gospel music performed by three little blind girls. You might think he'd be the silent type, that he'd never talk about Cyndy, that he would be ashamed of what she was.

But no. Every night he's not on duty, he's at the Blue Monkey, flirting with Cyndy's friends. The blue vine girls, as I think of them. They have tattoos of barbed wire around their wrists and ankles, like garlands of navy-blue flowers. There's Mari, the friendly one with a snaggle tooth; Gretchen, who would make such a good-looking boy, oh, Cyndy used to go nuts when I said that; and moody Heart, Cyndy's beloved, who tends bar. Heart wears sleeveless tops with tight silver jewelry high on her arms, glamorous. She makes lists of everybody she's ever known, Cyndy said, long spiraling lists on notebook paper. When she runs out of paper, she writes on her arm. Ed likes to lean across the bar and turn Heart's face toward him, raising her chin gently with his fingers. Her expression never changes; it's the look of somebody with so many names to write down, she'll never be finished.

When will he realize he's in love with her? I'm waiting, holding my breath. It's been six months since Cyndy died. I rarely go to the Blue Monkey with him; I just drive by slowly enough to see him lifting Heart's chin with his fingertips, night after night. If he leaves me, I'll be through with the supper club. Scandal is the only way out.

What can we do for Cyndy now, besides establish a scholarship fund in her name at the art school where she taught?

We've done that. Take the blue monkey home and plug it into the wall? Heart has a monkey, Cyndy told me, a small, bad-tempered one. Heart's deaf as a post, Cyndy said. She reads lips, memorizes what the regulars like to drink. The monkey knows she's deaf. He helps her live a normal life. When her doorbell rings or her telephone, he jumps up and down, tugs on her clothes, and beats his chest.

Cyndy was asleep in her apartment when the man climbed up to her balcony and slid back the glass door. He wore socks, no shoes. Slid back the door and went in.

THE THIRD- and fourth-floor windows at Cedar Mount are wide open, spring through fall, without screens. The house sits on the only hill in our little town, so that with its four stories, it looms far above the ground, too high for bugs or bats to be a problem. A tiny black cat lives in the fourth-floor bedroom. She's old, with tremors in her back legs and a harsh cry that makes kids say, "Halloween kitty." She's still playful, leaping from one twin bed to the other, in her high room. I like to think of her sleeping up there by herself, after the tourists have gone home.

Buddy's hand, holding mine beneath the supper club table at Cedar Mount, is the only thing anchoring me to earth. His wife, Dolly, serves the most glorious meal I've ever eaten: trout almondine, potatoes dauphinoise, a cake made with brandy. "New Orleans-style food," Dolly explains. She is always modest; I admire that. I worry about her and Buddy living in this house. All those steps, for one thing. Four stories' worth of stairs. Buddy's too heavy, and Dolly wears high heels all day, every day. It's part of her look, the high heels and her bun of gray hair, and a different suit every day of the year. I love this house and everything in it: a Victorian glass fishbowl bigger than any globe of the world; a sideboard Dolly claims was owned by Napoleon; a cheval mirror with the silver worn off so that looking into it, you have no feet, no top of head. Childless, they have beggared themselves buying antiques and preserving this mansion. The governor has dined here, and a former president. Dolly has a full-time housekeeper. She probably pays the housekeeper more than she earns herself.

They are better than I am, Dolly and Buddy. When they get old, how will they manage the stairs?

"Light the candleboard," Dolly instructs Buddy, and he shuffles into the front hallway with a box of long matches. The candleboard holds twenty-four candles at the level of the high glass transom over the massive door. This requires a stepladder. Supper over, we all go to watch him. He lights every candle. A surgeon and his wife steady the ladder. Mimsy says, "Don't fall," but he won't; he has lit the candleboard a thousand, ten thousand times. A hundred and sixty years ago, when this house was young, its owner required the candles lit every night he was away from it, so he could see his house from far off when he was riding home on horseback.

"That wouldn't work now," says Buddy, wheezing as he climbs down the ladder, recalling the story. "Too much light everywhere. It was darker then." This thought seems to please him, though he has told the story as often as he has lit the candles. He tells the story to all the tourists, and to his students when he brings them here. "Darker back then," he says, and retreats into that lonely space inside himself where I have known him to go after we've been together, in the seediest motels we can find within an hour's drive, with weeds in the courtyards and dry, gaping pools and the shrieks of children whose parents have left them there forever. He needs his own high-ceilinged rooms. I hate making him go to those motels, when he could be here at Cedar Mount, amid beauty, among highboys smelling of lemon oil, trays of French cut-glass decanters, no two alike, and the great glass globe with its single fantail fish.

Buddy and Ed and I have lived in this town all our lives. Of all the members of the supper club, we're the only ones who grew up and went to high school here. All the others moved here from somewhere else.

CYNDY NEVER had to come out to me. I knew from a certain way she stretched her arms over her head and flexed her shoulders when she yawned. Her early grasp of irony: somehow that, too, and the way, as a child, she loved the song "Clementine." *Oh my darling, oh my darling!*

"Mom, you look so young," she used to say.

"I was a child bride," I said, and we'd laugh, because I wasn't.

By the time she died, at twenty-five, she had hard wrinkles around her eyes and mouth. The wrinkles were beautiful. "Sculptors age fast," she said. "The stonecutters, you should hear them coughing. This one woman at the art school, she sounds like she's dying," she said proudly.

Cyndy was famous in that last year of her life, making enough money to take Heart on gambling trips, enough to rent the high-rise apartment where she was killed. Heart was the one who found her.

Cyndy wanted so much for them to live together. Heart wouldn't, because it would upset the monkey. Cyndy tried to make it work. She took Heart and the monkey for drives in the country. Cyndy loved the roads. Convicts' roads, she'd say, Indian trails. Heart would make her stop beside endless flat cornfields so the monkey could get out and do his business.

"I'm so hoping she'll lose that damn thing," Cyndy said. "Mom, I love her too much," and she cried, the deep lines around her mouth as old as stone. The monkey raced up and down the fields, pulling at the cornstalks, shrieking, while Heart and Cyndy chased him through the tall, rustling rows. He always came back.

"She might be making up names on those lists of hers," I told Cyndy.

"I thought of that a long time ago," Cyndy said, "and I don't care if she is."

The Blue Monkey was where they met, only it wasn't a bar then, it was an Italian restaurant. It's one of those buildings that has passed through many incarnations. Snow had fallen, rare for this part of Virginia, and the restaurant staff and customers were having a snowball fight out on the sidewalk. They were all into it, a young crowd, laughing, packing snowballs and hurling them at each other. Heart was a waitress. Cyndy was heading across the street to have lunch there. Then the commotion was over, fast, and the crowd scattered like cats do when they're done playing. Heart was the last one to go inside. She stood by herself, turning a snowball over and over in her hands.

I was Cyndy's business manager, keeping track of her projects and commissions. She made a lot of money and spent it fast, spent it all before she died, as if she knew.

"DOLLY, COULD I go upstairs and lie down, for just a little while?" I ask our hostess, who hears me with only half an ear. She can't refuse. To Ed I say, "You go ahead. Don't wait for me." He swings his short beard toward me, and behind his tinted glasses, he's as expressionless as Heart. I don't want him coming by later to pick me up, or worse yet, phoning.

I don't think he will.

From the stairs, I hear the evening end. All over town on this Saturday night, supper clubs are winding down.

"It was so lovely, scrumptious, perfect. Good night."

"Dolly, you are a genius, good night."

"Oh, thank you, dears, it was our pleasure. Be careful on the steps down to the sidewalk."

I worry about Buddy and Dolly every time it rains. Living on the only hill for miles around, they've got steep steps outside and in.

I keep on climbing. Their bedroom and the only bathroom are on the second floor. Guest quarters are on the third and fourth, but months go by when they don't have guests. By the third floor, there are no more sounds from anywhere, not from the front door, not from outside. By the fourth floor, there's only the mewing of the cat. She bounds toward me, leading the way into the dark room with its twin beds, mattresses on ropes. I know where everything is. I don't turn on any lights.

All I want is to sleep for a little while. Buddy won't come up; he probably doesn't even know I'm still here. He and Dolly will go to bed. The housekeeper must be washing the decanters and the Limoges plates as she has done so many times. The unscreened windows are open. Buddy was wrong. It's plenty dark around here. I'm above the treetops, and the trees alone block out the light. I ease off my shoes and stretch out on the narrow bed by the window, the cat in my arms. The pillows are dusty, as I hoped they would be, and the room smells faintly of the cat herself, fur and pee. This is all I want, to rest up here, to ride out far from town and circle back, the blazing candleboard a beacon to those on horseback. I could think about that for the rest of my life.

THE SIGN. Hours later, I wake up and remember I've got to go and pay the manager, unplug the famous blue neon monkey, and take it home. It must be three in the morning, or later. By now, my husband and Heart might be the only ones there.

The silver bands on Heart's arms will reflect the light from the big TV over the bar as she turns it off and closes up, Ed helping her. The sign will create an electrical smell when they unplug it, like a burn in the air.

But I stay where I am. I couldn't move if I wanted to. Morning will come, and I'll slip down all those stairs, and out the door with its original lock and key, and I'll keep on going.

The little cat beside me is so old, she could die any day. Buddy will grieve so, when she does. My hand covers her whole body. She twitches all over, dreaming. I don't believe the Blue Monkey is closing forever. Something else will open up there, in a few weeks, a few months, as if nothing had ever changed.

The Broken Lake

Forest Lodge
Glen Allen, Virginia
Spring 1903

AFTER A WEEK of hard, heavy rain, Castle Lake burst into Crystal Lake, and as one they split their banks and flooded out a section of railroad tracks big enough to hold an engine and twenty freight cars. The next morning, giddy sunshine threw its sparks over the receding water, violets and jill o' the ground bloomed in the spongy earth, a haze of gnats danced smokily above the shining shallow puddles, and Lizzie Fletcher opened the door of her uncle's hotel to greet the president of the RF&P Railroad, a man frantic for his enterprise.

She, who pushed her sharp cheekbones out at the world, one broken like a smooth bowl put together wrong, from the time in England when as a child she spun beneath the wheels of a gig: she loved this home of hers. She was easier with people than with critters, such as the peacocks that picked their way among the rose paths and came to peck the ground near Alexander Bean's feet. Lizzie distrusted peacocks; you could live with them for years and never win their cold glamorous blue love. Her uncle, Captain John Cussons, adored them all, the peacocks and turkeys and pheasants, geese and squirrels and muskrat, and most of all the deer that shoved their dumb gentle mouths into his hand and scratched their velvet antlers against his sleeve.

Lizzie had spent all morning gazing from a fourth-story window, the spyglass cold against her eye, enthralled by the marvel of damage. The railroad tracks and hapless freight cars zigzagged in a watery still life on her very lawn, their cargo of lumber and gravel spilled and afloat. She wished there were more guests to see the spectacle. Uncle John was rich, no matter that few visitors came to Forest Lodge. That hurt his touchy pride, which she protected as best she could. From her high window, she'd looked through the glass, past the angular question marks of the oaks' branches to the skewed deranged tracks. Gazing beyond the rail line, she focused on the homesteads she knew so well: Broaddus, Tinsley, Sheppard, big houses with lightning rods proud and green-globed against the sky; the modest huts of Steele, Black, Purcell, and Granger, whose inhabitants now stood gawking at the washout; and finally she fixed the glass on the deep secret spot in the woods where Melton lived, Melton whom her uncle hated, and for a long time, so had she. He had killed a fawn. He couldn't read.

In the far distance, Richmond offered a vibrant purple glow to her vision, a silver energy, as if the rails and the new violets converged in crazed profusion.

The immediate danger was past. Last night the rail offices had been notified by telegraph, telephone, and hysterical messenger, and Uncle John wrote in his huge script to the railroad president: "Accept my hospitality, Sir, while we negotiate settlement for this misfortune."

So she opened the door to a gamine-faced man whom right away she wanted to torment. "If you're here to sell soap or gold mines, why don't you go on down to Melton's. He needs a gold mine."

"Ma'am," the man said and took off his hat. "Is Captain Cussons at home?"

"You must be Alexander Bean," she said, bringing him into the foyer.

She was thirty that spring, and when her uncle died in 1912 she would inherit it all: the hotel and the deer park, the printing shop and the thousand acres, and with her hundred thousand dollars she would sail to France. Newspapermen writing the Captain's obituary got Lizzie's kinship all balled up. Was she niece to her uncle or her aunt? She could have told them she was her uncle's niece by blood, not Aunt Susan's, Aunt Susan who was so much older than John Cussons, Susan who died of a stroke the day after a terrible storm swept through in 1896, Susan who had been married for her money! Though nobody ever said so.

So Lizzie said, "Come in" to Alexander Bean and watched with pride while his cider-colored eyes took in the huge foyer, the paintings all over the walls (a feathery Virginia crane, Uncle on horseback, an Alpine ravine), and the double stairway that swept upwards, capped by eagle finials. Alexander Bean was handsome except for his short square teeth that reminded her of a nutcracker's. Yet she felt a physical warmth for him and was glad for the flood. She had heard the lake break, "as if the earth were changing its mind," she said as she showed Alexander Bean to his room, where within the hour they became lovers, her uncle being gone across the village to visit the schoolteacher, Miss Polly, and all the servants and villagers being gathered out in the yard to exclaim about the tracks and to say how quiet it was without the sharp shrill whistle and the screaming wheels of the trains whose times of passing they knew by heart, for by now the RF&P line had been down for twelve hours and the people of Glen Allen pricked up their ears at the silence. It was March, too early for towhees, yet there they sounded (*swingalee swingalee swingalee*) and the *kipkipkip* of the grasshopper sparrow, even the sleepy *kleer!* of the flicker, that you heard only in deep August, on afternoons when you were trying not to fall asleep. Work at the print shop of Cussons, May and Company was suspended. Captain Cussons was off at the schoolhouse, which was located in Miss Polly's upstairs living room, trying to convince her to teach in a real schoolhouse, which he himself would pay for and build, just so the students would quit tumbling down the stairs and using up all of Dr. Winfrey's slings and splints. Careless wild things, children. The Captain and his wife had produced only one baby, Athenase, who died so young. Susan had been a little too old when they were married, and though she'd been married before, to Benjamin Allen, a rough old cuss who took a long time dying, she had no children by Benjamin either. Her father, old Mosby Sheppard, had made her marry Benjamin, she'd said. By the time she died, she had got so quiet, Susan had, that nothing seemed to reach her but the peacocks.

"I feel good," said Alexander Bean, eyes shut, smiling up at the whitewashed sunlight on the ceiling of the room John Cussons was letting him have for free. His bags were still downstairs in the reception hall and Lizzie said she'd have Galilee bring them up, but Galilee was outside with his shirt off, shouting. She could hear him; there'd be no calling him in from the sight of the rail lines being hauled back into place, of workmen with shovels and hoes churning the muddy swath with concern and glee.

"You're not calling anybody to bring them up," said Alexander Bean, drawing her to him. The rumpled sleigh bed with its white sheets was one where Lizzie often slept herself. Forest Lodge had a hundred rooms. She could choose whichever one she liked; she had her own private suite and her pick of scores of others. Hardly a soul came out to drink the sulphurous waters of the healthful springs or to eat in the huge dining room or watch the plays that John Cussons staged in the auditorium with the heavy gold curtains and, at Christmastime, wreaths of holly and running cedar. He had built too close to the tracks, and guests would dart half awake into the hallways in their nightclothes, shrieking from the ferocious noise of the hurtling trains, which jolted them from slumber and sent them into nervous rages. They would pack their trunks at three in the morning and head out, hysterical and heedless, while John Cussons followed them in his rippling nightshirt and the gauntlets he always wore in winter, his boots hastily pulled onto his tree-trunk legs, cajoling and soothing. It often worked with women. They melted back into their rooms, soft, protesting wraiths, their paths lit by gas lanterns, and in the morning accepted doses of chalybeate and lithia water, then hilariously strolled the garden with the Captain after a lunch of roast chicken, fried perch, and sweet potato pie. He kept candied orange peel in his pockets, for deer and ladies.

Alexander Bean didn't seem to be thinking about his ruined rail line at all. He asked who else was staying at the hotel and allowed Lizzie to lead him to the window, where, wrapped in a sheet, she pointed out to him the other guests: a dentist from Norfolk, who snored and had vile breath; a fierce old gentleman from Kilmarnock, taking the cure for catarrh with his equally aged wife and body servant; twin young ladies from Washington who rarely left their rooms; and a thin, evasive boy whom Lizzie had reason to fear, for he had seen her with Melton, in the woods. She had spied the boy's bright bumpy face flashing through the leaves as Melton ran his hands over her neck. These people she identified to Alexander Bean. They were all down by the tracks, even the haughty twins from Washington, one of whom had not even bothered to put on her bustle and who leaned with ridiculous concentration over a patch of mire where a red-jacketed laborer struggled to put the tracks to rights.

Alexander Bean clicked his nutcracker teeth and murmured something about calling the chief of conductors. The scent of his skin was on her skin, yet they were strangers, and if they met every day in this bed, they'd be strangers still, Lizzie believed. That was how it was if you started out fast. She stayed passionate, she was a passionate woman. Years later, after her uncle's death, living in Paris in the fantastic house that was supported by the fabulous accounts her brokers arranged for her, she started a love affair in the Bois de Boulogne simply by answering a question with a question. "Are you Chantal?" the man would say. "And what if I were?" she'd answer. He would be a Spaniard, and he was unknown to Lizzie as she crouched by Alexander Bean's window, her fast breathing slowing down a beat at a time.

Alexander Bean talked a lot. He showed her photographs from a trip to China. He had pictures of the bound feet of an aristocratic Chinese woman, "deformed," he said, "into a lotus hook. They find it very beautiful," and together they mouthed disgust at the poor bent flesh of the Chinese woman, the horrible pity of her broken toes and hobbled heel, until Lizzie realized he must have made love with that woman, and then she went into herself again, remembering with satisfaction how the lake had sounded when it broke, causing all this trouble for Alexander Bean's railroad. She had known the flood was coming, of course, known it was serious; legions of small wild animals had sought the high ground as the gray rain drummed a reproach on the fifty thousand square feet of the rooftops of Forest Lodge.

She had known the lakes would never last. Uncle John was proud that they were man-made, spring-fed, "could be drained off within twenty-four hours and leave not a drop of stagnant water," yet she'd always sensed a seismic power there, a liquid rebellion in those deep and shallow cups to which he gave such fanciful names: Castle Lake, Crystal Lake, Echo Lake, Hidden Lake, and most remote, to which she hardly ever went, Lake of the Woods. He who had lived with the Sioux, whom the Indians named Wau-zee-hos-ka, the Tall Pine Tree, he who had scouted for Generals Bee, Whiting, and Law, he who had met his wife while running from the Yankees—he'd found shelter in Susan's farmhouse, under the bed where Benjamin Allen lay dying. Years later, in Paris, Lizzie will receive calls over the transatlantic cable from journalists wanting to know was it true a band of braves had stayed at Forest Lodge? And Sitting Bull? And she'll tell them what she can remember of the dark-faced black-haired men who were so quiet that even when you passed them on the stairs, you might have been alone. She'll make things up, of course— that they were wild, that they danced on the roof. She will fall asleep in her mint-green bed and let the telephone dangle beside it, the phone's transatlantic gurgle going soft as falling snow.

But the day of the lake was years before, when she was young, when she had just lain with Alexander Bean and felt, with a rippling flush on her skin, that he wasn't so easily dismissed as the others. She forgot Melton's urgent mouth. She could have watched her uncle shoot him to avenge the dead fawn (consumed with buttermilk gravy, Melton had told her), watched unblinking. She pulled on her green dress and raked her fingers through her hair. Alexander Bean wanted to call the chief of conductors, who was down in Blacksburg, "and I'll tell him everything'll be fine by morning."

Lizzie laughed. Everything would be fine just by dint of the water seeping into the earth, and all Alexander Bean had done was show her some photographs of stunted feet, while his workmen toiled down below. "You can use the telephone in my uncle's office," she said.

She led him down to the office and left him there, then went outside, past the oaks, down the rose path through the black-and-silver entrance gates of Forest Lodge. Water soaked through her shoes. The thought of dinner crossed her mind, the fact that all these people would need to eat, guests and laborers and lookers-on, and she should go to the kitchen and see to the supplies of ham and rice and gravy. They had strawberries from Gloucester, and a bushel of fresh oysters.

There was her uncle with Miss Polly hanging on his arm (dry as a biscuit, sharp as old cheese), and nearby was his friend Polk Miller, author of a book on canine diseases and treatments. In a crowd, she always flew to him; he was gentle.

Caw, caw, caw! Crows wheeled in from the pine woods and settled on an abandoned boxcar. It seemed to Lizzie, waving gnats away from her face, that they rocked with delight at the human commotion. Polk Miller touched Lizzie's arm and directed her attention to a minnow flashing in the grass, a hardy escapee.

Then Lizzie saw the woman.

This woman had come quietly down Mountain Road, leading a child by the hand, joining the group around the tracks at the farthest edge. In the child's fleshy piratical scowl, Lizzie saw Melton. This woman had preceded Lizzie in his warm hard clasp and now crept about the village as furtive as a fox, glimpsed sometimes at dawn or twilight, and now in full daylight appearing to Lizzie's eyes as out of place as an owl. Across the glare of water, she regarded Lizzie with wide eyes and lips parted as if she were about to speak. Lizzie knew her only as "Miss Shaw," and Melton had never said a word about her. Lizzie moved her gaze from Miss Shaw to the child, small and black-browed; she looked again at the child's mother, and Miss Shaw opened her mouth and sang.

Sang: and the crowd stilled and turned to stare at her. Workmen swiveled around with their shovels in midair. Children stopped their games of tag and leaned unblinking toward her. She sang an old song about rain and water that Lizzie didn't know. It was an American song, and Lizzie hated Miss Shaw for the song and for her voice, even as she yearned toward that clear sailing pitch that reached the corners of the village and deep into the woods. "My God," said Polk Miller under his breath. The thin evasive boy, one of the hotel guests, stood slack-jawed, and the twin ladies from Washington looked at each other, then at Miss Shaw, then back again at each other as if seeing the other for the first time. The fierce old gentleman from Kilmarnock took off his hat and held it over his heart, leaning on his servant.

The villagers were slow to move, as if Miss Shaw's beautiful voice had stunned them. George May, one of the partners in the printing business, mouthed the words of the song as Miss Shaw sang them. Big Bessie Tinsley raised her arms slowly, as if about to conduct an orchestra. Mary Collier began to cry, Chester Broaddus closed his eyes and seemed to pray, and Lizzie heard somebody murmur: *She lives in the first story of a house that's all burned out abovestairs, out on Courtney Road.*

Lizzie looked for Melton but didn't see him. For the first time, she wondered if the lake had damaged anybody's home, if the washout on the tracks were only part of something worse. She could ask Polk Miller. She pictured Melton's little hut bobbing about in a swamp, but the high soaring notes of Miss Shaw's song went all the way to the sun, and it was hard to think at all. Miss Shaw's brown hair fell to her shoulders in loose brushy waves, thick as paintbrushes at the ends, and her shoulders were almost bare. Lizzie had known about Miss Shaw and the baby, as surely as if it were written in the sky. She had hoped Miss Shaw would leave. At other times, she'd pictured Miss Shaw stealing to the steps of Forest Lodge and leaving the baby on the porch for Lizzie to raise. No, Lizzie wouldn't want it. The child was just old enough to walk, yet looked as if he could aim a gun and shoot you through the neck.

Miss Shaw's voice climbed higher, she put her hand to her breast as if to push the notes out of her lungs, and from her full red lips came her human music. The last bars of song arced and wavered and sank, like sparks flaring and going out. Everybody listened to the silence as they had listened to her sing, and then Miss Shaw turned her child by his shoulders and led him back up Mountain Road, the ribbons on her sleeves fluttering in the breeze that had sprung up. The surface of the easing flood quivered in tiny wavelets. Miss

Shaw's dress was a pink smudge that Lizzie followed with her eyes until it was gone. She wondered if the burned house still smelled of ashes, like a fireplace.

"Polk," she said, "was anybody hurt by the flood?"

"Oh yes," he said, his eyes stretching at her. "Didn't you know, my dear?" and he pointed in various directions of the village. The lakes had boiled, slopped over, reached their watery fingers into people's very beds.

"They'll hate us more," Lizzie said. "Polk, my uncle's been so good to them, but they'll blame us for this. They blame my uncle for everything." She felt rage toward the villagers in their wet, drafty houses, all those who had suffered in the night of water. She saw that Polk Miller barely heard her.

"That girl," he said to Chester Broaddus at his elbow. "Lord, Lord," and the two men rubbed their mouths.

"Makes me feel like gettin' drunk," Chester Broaddus said, and they laughed.

"Was anybody swept away by it?" Lizzie asked Polk. "By the flood. Anybody drowned?"

He shook his head. She wanted to recall him from the spell Miss Shaw had cast. She was relieved when he cleared his throat and started telling George Broaddus about a child up in Ashland who had died from the bite of a rabid dog. He'd invented a cure for just about anything could go wrong with dogs, Polk said, except when they went mad. Surely the fix was in the earth somehow, in a plant or the bark of a tree.

Painfully, the rails were aligned again, only to float out of place. Alexander Bean, who bounded down the hotel steps and strode to the disaster, declared that new fill dirt must be brought in, the ground was a sponge, the tracks would never hold, you couldn't expect them to bear the weight of a train. He consulted with workmen and engineers. They cast about for dry earth and sent a wagon and a team of horses up Mountain Road toward higher ground.

"Who's he?" Bessie Tinsley asked Lizzie. Bessie's hairdo reminded Lizzie of the Great Sphinx. Uncle John had pictures of the Sphinx in his office, and he and Lizzie often debated was it smiling?

"The railroad president," Lizzie said automatically, and as her lips formed the words she realized what pleasure it gave her to say them. "The chief of the RF&P."

"And he's staying with you?" Bessie asked, her Sphinx-head dipping coyly.

"He is," said Lizzie. Bessie was one of the few village women who would speak to her. The others resented her and her uncle and so did their men, except for those whom he'd made rich, like the Sheppards, who were Aunt Susan's people, and an Allen or two, the last of the died-out line from Susan's first husband. Again Lizzie looked for Melton. She was glad he hadn't heard Miss Shaw's song. She herself could not sing. Her voice was a rusty chain, hoarse always; to make up for that she always spoke low. She wondered if Bessie Tinsley hated her and her uncle. Lake of the Woods had claimed Bessie's son Tom in January of '98. The lake was frozen hard, and children went skating. One midnight a warm spell came through, and the ice split open and swallowed Tom. His sister came screaming up to Forest Lodge. With torches the men went and ringed the lake. In silence they jerked his body from the fissured ice and wiped the leaves from his face.

Lizzie was thirty; she knew she did not look it. She thought little of her life in England. She could have stayed in Lincolnshire and tatted lace in her mother's house forever. She was glad she'd come here when Aunt Susan got sick, and was not sorry that Aunt Susan was dead. She had never understood Aunt Susan and they'd never gotten along.

Uncle John came and found her. Was dinner ready, he wanted to know.

"I'll see to it," Lizzie said.

Uncle John waved Alexander Bean over. Was Mr. Bean pleased with his room?

"Very nice," said Alexander.

Her uncle's big shoulders blotted out the sun. Yes, said Alexander Bean, it was a fine hotel. Lizzie smiled at her uncle, squinting at his haloed head. Every night they read a portion of Dickens together and laughed till their cheeks ached at the hinges. She could serve plates of clay for dinner and he would still call her his lamb.

How much John Cussons knew—he who had lived with Indians! They gashed the corpses, red men did, the corpses of their rivals; from the marks you could tell which tribe had won. Lizzie had learned the marks from him. Uncle John knew the women's dirge for their own who died. He knew how winter felt in the West. He didn't say much about the terrible war of secession—he who was scout, sharpshooter, soldier of the line. Mention Appomattox and he'd tell you, "General Lee didn't offer his sword, and Grant didn't ask for it." Uncle John, who was master of thespians at Point Lookout prison, host and entertainer even under enemy guard!

Making her way to the kitchen, Lizzie caught Alexander Bean's eye and smiled. She'd never believed she had to wait for a man in order for her life to begin. Yet she would spend hours on beauty. You could put belladonna in your eyes, eat arsenic to whiten your skin, spend half a day with your hair rolled up, yet never, ever look pretty enough.

Alexander Bean turned away when someone called him. One of the men.

Lizzie went in the kitchen and scolded Rose for not putting the okra and black-eyed peas on sooner. She sent Rose's daughter to get Galilee to shuck the oysters. The pans of yeast rolls made her mouth water. She buttered a roll and ate it. When the food was hot and on the table, she went out and waved to her uncle. He led them in, the hungry workmen and the guests, leaving only the villagers outside with the staccato crying of the crows.

"Who was that woman who sang?" Alexander Bean asked as he followed her into the dining room.

"They call her Miss Shaw," she said, and she couldn't swallow a bite after that.

While they were eating, a woman swept in, businesslike, and John Cussons made a fuss over her, "Miss Edyth Beveridge, the photographer," and had her sit next to him, crowding Miss Polly, the schoolteacher, who grimly spooned stewed tomatoes into her mouth. Miss Polly was furious about the flood. This was the day John Cussons had promised to drive her out to Yellow Tavern, where poor Jeb Stuart had lost his life, yet the whole day had been taken up with rail lines. She turned a bitter ear to the engineers, stalwarts of the RF&P, with their talk of rolling stock and iron.

Miss Beveridge would photograph the scene of the flood, John Cussons announced. The engineers fell over themselves, Lizzie thought, to offer to help her, though Miss Beveridge was far past her prime. The chief engineer had some experience with cameras, he said, so he would handle her picture-making things with his own careful hands, and Miss Beveridge through her tiny round spectacles favored him with a smile. Wasn't it a beautiful day, she asked.

"Oh yes," the men cried, outdoing each other in their fervor.

"I only notice sunlight for my work anymore," Edyth Beveridge said to John Cussons and sighed, and Miss Polly speared a pickle from the dish with a vicious stroke.

Through loblolly pine and stands of post oak, Lizzie rushed after dinner, through sumac, box elder, ash. She could not wait any longer. It seemed to her that she still heard Miss Shaw's leaping soprano, saw her white throat pulsing. She caught her shoe on a rope of old grapevine as thick and gray as an elephant's trunk and pitched forward, struck her head on a rock, and lay still on the forest floor.

She was eighteen and there was James Early, the miller's son, asking her to be his wife. She laughed at him. Oh, you'll never get married now, you cruel girl, her mother said, tears spurting from her eyes as James Early let the door fall shut and Lizzie sank back in her window seat, her laughter drying to a sneeze. James Early went on to marry a mean widow. His wife had twins, a boy and a girl, and they named them after themselves. Lizzie's eyes fluttered open. She saw a little snake beside the rock, a green one. Uncle John said they would drink milk from a cup, he said he'd had a pet snake one time, that it was cool to the touch. Somewhere she'd heard that a snake could suckle on a woman at night, sliding in a heavy coil over a new mother's ribs to her milky breasts.

Lizzie sat up and rubbed her head. She was close to one of the springs they didn't use much, a sweet cold one, and parting the bushes beside it (spirea, greening up to bloom), she bent her head and drank. She wasn't hurt, only dizzy. She balanced herself and ran again, and when she neared Melton's house deep in the woods, she cried his name, but all that came out was a rasp: "Clifford!"

No smoke from his chimney and a moat around the house, the last of the flood. Pinecones floated on the still surface. She stepped across the water and pushed his door open. "Clifford." Mice scurried away as she entered. The dirty window glass gave dim light. There was his bedsack, soaked on the floor. She had a sudden, terrible conviction that he was dead.

From the cupboard she took his whiskey bottle and drank a deep hard pull. If she lived here and not in the big white hundred-room hotel, she'd be a hunter's wife, a drunk's girl, a poacher's wench. It was sultry in the house, but there was no fire, and as she put the whiskey bottle down, she felt light and glad. She went back through the trees, startling a doe and a fawn, sent them bounding back to their windbreak, the shelter Uncle John had built for his beloveds. She reached the railroad. There was Miss Beveridge with her picture-making equipment. How hot the sun was, and what a crazy angle it made with its queer neap nearness. The back of Lizzie's neck was hot and her new dress torn at the hem. Her shoe had a barberry branch sticking out of the laces. She leaned down and fixed it, tasting whiskey on her tongue.

The sun had moved, spreading its light over the wide dazzling shine of the flood. Miss Beveridge bent her practiced head to the camera while the legs of the tripod sank into the mud, and three or four men rushed to assist her, moving her things to a safer place. People were besotted by the flood and the sudden sun. Lizzie wondered if the veterans would march. Old men marched these days for no reason at all. They'd bring out bunting and heft their bayonets and fall into line. Of course her uncle wasn't old, though he was sixty-five. Her heart ached to see his friends die. So many mornings he'd go off to Richmond and ride in a black procession, down Monument Avenue to Albemarle Street and up the little lanes of Hollywood Cemetery, laying somebody else to rest, and he'd come home with the smell of lilies in his clothes, tired, all day keeping the beat of the funeral songs in his step. Lizzie would serve him cake and ice cream, would send Galilee out to pick bunches of grapes to cheer him up. To see Uncle John with his great head bent—nothing wrenched her the way his sorrow did.

Now, at the flooded place, she searched for his big shape and saw in it his habitual joy, the pleasure of a man meant for naming things, giving commands, and restoring order. He rode his gray horse Buck, patrolling the lines of railroad men as they cast their ropes about the strewn sections of track and, grunting, hauled them into place. The floodwaters sloshed in waves as the long metal rails resisted. Uncle John's long hair leaped on his back. She wondered how many men he'd killed and if he dreamed about them. He had sent bullets into the bodies of men, had lived beyond them to make love, to grow hungry and satisfied for years and years since the war was over.

These days Lizzie herself was always hungry; she'd go into the kitchen and help herself to cold meat and figs and cheese. She kept biscuits in her pocket. She took one out now and nibbled it while her feet turned toward the hotel again, wanting Alexander Bean because she couldn't find Melton. His empty house. She pictured him at Miss Shaw's burned shelter, and it maddened her. She pictured him holding the child on his knee and running his hand over Miss Shaw's round buttocks, and the biscuit in her mouth went dry with rage. She wished Miss Shaw had died in the fire, that her big breasts and thick brown hair were melted and gone to wax and vapor and ash.

To look at the crowd by the tracks, to hear their shouts, you'd think they were drunk, all of them. Polk Miller waved to her from far down the flood, the water reflecting his pale trousers in a long shine. She wondered if some loose train, uninformed, would hurtle from the sunny holes at either end of the tracks, north and south, would come smashing into the crowd and destroy them. What would Alexander Bean say? He wouldn't get hurt. Men like him never did. He'd watch it and be shaken and would find somebody to blame, and after awhile he wouldn't think about it anymore. The crowd milled in its zone of light, and the sunlight on the sweeping, still floodwaters was silver fire.

Hungry, she went inside the hotel and found Alexander Bean picking out a tune on the piano. Miss Shaw's song. She recognized the notes. She hated them both. She stood behind him, knocking biscuit crumbs from her lips, smoothing burrs from her skirt, until he turned around and looked up at her. With a shock she realized how young he was—younger than she was, just a boy who'd come into the railroad presidency and now played music while his tracks sank into a new sea. Fine lines creased his freckled forehead, and his red-gold hair waved back from his temples. He clicked his nutcracker teeth at her. He was too young to have fought in the war or even been born then. He'd never killed anybody. His clothes had cost a lot of money. He reached out and caught her around the waist and together they went down the hallway toward the auditorium, where on the stage, behind the curtain, they lay down on a pile of carpets and tickled each other.

A dumber man she wouldn't have gone with. Alexander Bean was smart; that always did it for her. She'd been with other men, other guests, enough now that she did not remember all their names, but always they were men who had seen something of the world and carried its many rhythms in their heads. She could discern this. Now their tickling hands, hers and Alexander's, went under their clothes, and they tossed their outer things off and stripped down to their underneath things, there on the stacked Oriental rugs with their musty woolen smell and the dust of the curtain making her cough. The curtain was a great gold velvet affair trimmed with silk tassels of hunter's green. The place was as compelling to her as Alexander Bean's body, even as he reached for her.

His hands were strong. She knew the prints of his fingers and thumbs would be marked in bruises on her upper arms. She talked to him as he touched her, she spoke in her low voice, and it was Melton she wanted, Melton who couldn't read and had given a frowning little boy to Miss Shaw, so poor she lived in a burned-out house.

She felt Alexander Bean sit up and look at her, but her eyes were too heavy to open. When at last she opened them, she saw that Alexander Bean was crying. His tears falling on her shoulders and chest were hot as tar. He gathered her to him and said, "Oh, Lizzie."

For a long time they lay there, just behind the gold curtain, and she was aware of the hundred wooden seats beyond the stage, empty and expectant chairs, worn by the posteriors of guests who had never responded quite enthusiastically enough to Uncle John's plays and musicales. At last she moved away from Alexander. Through the thick walls and passageways of the hotel came the distant cries of the workers and merrymakers at the flood, and from nearby, at a thin glass window off the wings of the stage, she heard the song of a cardinal perched on a pine limb: "Joking Joe! Joking Joe! Joking, joking, joking Joe!"

"Roll me up in a rug," she told Alexander Bean, and he tucked her into one end of a carpet with a design of vines and flowers and tightly wound it around her, rolling her over and over into a long, packaged cylinder, a human cigarette with her hair a lit flame at the end. It felt wonderful. Her breasts pressed against her sore arms. Alexander's tears had dried and his face was once more that of the railroad president.

He unrolled her forcefully. Her body was a mummy, a wheel, something runaway in hard wool, her limbs taut, her face flat against the floor, then whipping into air. At last she lay naked on the far side of the rug, all the breath knocked out of her. She laughed into her hair. Alexander watched while she sat up and rested her forehead on her knees.

"You'd better go see to your tracks," she said. She was jarred from head to heels, her body a tuning fork ringing. Once he left, she heard his footsteps clicking up the aisle past the hundred empty chairs, and she lay down again on the rug and rested until she felt all right.

She had to know. In her third-floor room, as she bathed and put on fresh clothes and sturdy shoes, she didn't plan, she only felt. She was glad she had two good feet to walk on, not like the lame Chinese woman whom Alexander Bean had held in his arms; she bet he hadn't cried over her. She slipped down the back stairs and out the door and headed for Courtney Road.

She passed the store, where you could buy meat, flour, cloth, and nails. Its yard was crowded with wagons and horses, but the riders were all down at the flood, and the horses whickered as she went by. Everyone was out of their houses. She could have gone in anybody's home and set it afire, stolen their secret things. Mountain Road stretched east and west, and west she went as far as the corner that marked Courtney

Road, her shoes already ruined by mud. Here and there the creeks had split their banks, washing over the road in bright deep pools that stirred to life the small quick lives in the earth. She found tadpoles coaxed to motion right there in the water on the road, black-tailed dots swimming to the surface and down again, and nobody saw her except an old man on a distant porch, who, with his dog and his gun by his side, held her in his sights and did not salute.

Burned out above the first floor: there it was, Miss Shaw's house, sorry-looking as a wound, its stucco stained with soot, its roof a thin dry bat's wing with great holes where the fire had cut, its second-story windows blown. The yard offered shrubs that Lizzie loved: pearlbush, flowering quince, beauty-bush, grancy graybeard, ladders-to-heaven, chaste tree. The hitching post was singed and withered to a matchstick. Shards of glass lay in the green grass, burnt timbers bristled with nails, and she could smell char.

There she saw them: two bodies in the gloom, one clothed, one whitely naked, and in leaping rage she bent closer and perceived them as mother and son. Mother bathing son, in-side the burnt house. Miss Shaw set her boy in the washtub and poured water from a kettle over him, soaping him with a rag, while he splashed droplets onto his mother's pink dress. The ribbons at her elbows hung limp with water. She washed her son, and Lizzie backed away ashamed, hugging her arms against her chest as she leaned against the dirty boards of the house, and slow as an old woman crept off the porch and walked home.

"A BOATING party!" Miss Beveridge cried, snapping her cam-eras shut and beaming at John Cussons, including in her ec-stasy the four men who vied to carry her equipment into the hotel. "Yes, right away, before we lose any more of this wonderful water."

Uncle John held out his arms to Lizzie and she stood within his protection, feeling as thin and beaten as a stalk, and over her head, her uncle and Miss Beveridge worked out a contract by which Miss Beveridge would photograph the interior of Forest Lodge—the dining room, music room, and stage. It had been a great day for that lady, Lizzie gathered; she had her pictures of the flood and now she would collect a fine fee for future work. "My pictures are the food of my soul," Miss Beveridge declared, "and you, Captain, should be photographed too." She stepped back and with her hands made a frame of the Captain's face.

"We'll do it," said John Cussons, and Miss Beveridge marched triumphantly off, calling, "Boating party!"

"We're going to Lake of the Woods," said Uncle John, holding Lizzie gently in the circle of his arms. He raised her chin with his palm. She couldn't speak. "We're lucky nobody died," he said. "I'm giving Miss Beveridge and Mr. Bean and the ladies from Washington a ride to the lake."

"I'll catch up with you," Lizzie said. He let her go, and she watched him settle the guests in a wagon, including the old gentleman with catarrh, who seemed magically cured, and she turned away toward the boxcars, her heart beating hard. She had the idea Melton might be in one of them, asleep on the hard bare floor or on top of a load of coal—"black diamonds," the men called it. She slid open the doors of the boxcars, those that weren't locked, and peered inside, calling his name softly into the sooty chambers. He must have abandoned his watery house, sought shelter somewhere else. He would have slept all morning through the tumult, through

Miss Shaw's song (she hoped), unless he half woke and believed he heard an angel. She didn't find him.

A railroad man came over to her. She liked his sturdy brown boots and merry eyes, but he couldn't help her. She would go to the lake and join the others. She circled around the shrinking flood, the ruined tracks, and headed for the woods. The humid air felt like summer, and there was heat under her arms and all through her clothes.

What she wanted most of all, she already had: the sound of wind in the afternoon, the floral scent of nighttime rain, a life lived privately, nearly alone; breeze and rain enjoyed from the wide porches of her uncle's hotel. He'd carved their paradise from "pine barrens and crawfish flats," he'd proudly say, from land that Stoneman, Kilpatrick, and Sheridan had raided. Earlier soldiers had been here too, years ago—Lafayette had hitched his horse to the big red oak by an old tavern down the road. She thought of the soldiers whenever rain fell on Mountain Road, sheets of rain folding and bending into the road and the green grass, sharp stilettos marching and dancing on the ground. Mountain Road went far. You could go west all the way to Charlottesville, and up into the hills.

What she wanted, she had much of: a million leaves, green as hope in summer, brown as earth in wintertime, swirling in the November sky that was her favorite time of year. She loved the Virginia dirt, the hard gray ridged clamshells in the clay, old as the stars. Once the birds that flew above the Tidewater cast terrible scaly shadows with their reptile wings; then the waters dried up, pulled back, lapsed into tame rivers, creeks, swamps. She thought of the old waters as she picked her way through the woods, reaching a place so quiet she heard no human voices anymore, nothing but the birds up in the trees and the slipping motion of water sinking into earth.

It was still a tidal land. The moon pulled hard on it. She could think back and count her summers by the lovers she'd taken, these years in Virginia. She would take them, then let them go. Over in England, in the smoky dirt lanes of Lincolnshire, James Early must think of her less and less. He had his mill and his mean-faced wife; he had ground tons of flour and meal by now; the years rattled by like grains of corn sifting into the floor of his barn. James Early's face came back to her: his downturned eyes, his cleft chin, his blunt sorrow when she refused him. The memory hurt her for the first time, hard, and she stopped there in the woods, her shoes in hand, getting over it.

She had persimmon trees, she had all her life and all her time, her fires were banked. She never had to explain a thing. Uncle John knew, and he let her stay. They adored each other. He had his lovers, she guessed; she counted them sometimes, dreamed of them, hid her chuckles about Miss Polly; and she had hers. They had the sweet wind; they neither of them let a lover interfere with their hours on the long leaf-strewn verandah, while he tapped out his pipe on the railing and Lizzie sewed.

Lizzie's best lovers were men who had traveled. They told her things, brought their stories to her. Back in deep winter, a frontiersman who'd been all the way to San Francisco had told her about mandrake roots, the way they changed in your grasp, screaming as you pulled them from the ground. "Stretch your hand out on the map as far as it will go," that man had told her, "and that'll be California."

She broke through the beeches near Lake of the Woods, swollen far beyond its boundaries, and took in the sight of the rowboats full of guests. Her uncle was in his favorite, the *Fleur de Lys,* with several ladies. The boats slid over the silky black forest water, nudging against the trunks of trees. The lake was deep in the middle, deeper now in flood. This was the lake that had claimed Tom Tinsley. Cold and ice had stopped his breath.

Within the year, Lizzie's rival would be dead: in February 1904, Miss Shaw went out and laid her head on the tracks, and her people from a far corner of Chesterfield came and took her little boy away. But that afternoon, Friday, March 6, 1903, Lizzie stepped into a rowboat with Alexander Bean, and she was happy. Looking over the side of the boat, she saw her reflection in the water, lit by what sun could reach through the thick woods.

"Are you going to live here forever?" Alexander said, turning his oar so the boat moved in slow wide circles.

Until my uncle dies, she thought, but that hurt too much to say. "You should stay with us a while longer," she said, and smiled at him. Her heart reached past him and fastened on the woods where Melton lived. If he'd gone away, she might never see him again. She turned away from that thought and planned a supper menu in her mind: quail, ham, salsify, butterbeans. Alexander Bean should marry somebody middle-aged and mule-eared, she decided, as a way of letting go of him, someone who would scold and soothe him and make his favorite chutneys.

She watched her uncle row his boatful of women to the bank, tie up the boat, and stroll into the woods. She heard them laughing in the forest. The others, too, pulled up their boats and went ashore, so Lizzie and Alexander were alone.

All afternoon the birds had called as if it were summertime: the yellow warbler and the yellowthroat, the jay, bobwhite, cardinal, and the incessant crows. Dusk drew on, chilly. Lizzie remembered that it was only March after all, and early in the month; it had been a false spring.

Alexander rowed toward land. He edged the boat into shallow water, stepped out, and steadied the boat so she could get out. "Watch your feet," he warned, but she didn't care that they got wet. He pulled her to him. When he kissed her, she thought of Melton. The earth smelled cold and fresh, and Alexander's face was warm.

"It's so quiet," Alexander said. His eyes looked puzzled and sad.

"No trains running," said Lizzie. The silence stretched out, the way it must have before the tracks were ever built, when the Indians hunted at the creek with their arrowheads of quartz and chert. She kept waiting for that low locomotive thunder, the whistle that shrieked its speed, but she heard only Alexander's heartbeat as she leaned against his chest, and a muffled wind that could have been owls' wings sweeping over them.

She stepped back. "You go ahead," she told him. "I just want to listen."

He shook his head, jammed his hands into his pockets, and left her. The soft blue dusk made the lake look dark. She knelt beside it, stirring the water with a reed, and saw in the shallows an undulating snake—a live rope, a black whip. Flick: it was gone, and the water held only the sky.

The Iron Road

BRANDY MADE HERSELF small as a rabbit to crawl beneath the freight car. It was cool and dark there, a good place to hide. She clutched the wooden ties of the tracks, scratching her hands, and found a penny which she held outside the freight car's shadow to inspect, then slipped into the pocket of her dress. She didn't mind how cramped and sooty her place was. She was delighted to disobey her mother and father, who constantly told her not to go too close to the tracks or the cars that sometimes sat idle, like this one, waiting to be hitched to an engine of the Norfolk Southern or the Chessie System and highball down to the Southern mountains or up to the big cities of the North. Stay away from there, her mother always said, stay close to the house.

Brandy had gotten as far as this safe shadow beneath the freight car, and she curled up as best she could and peered out from it. There was her house, solid and blue, its lightning rods piercing the low sky. Close by, on the other side of the tracks, was an old hotel, built after the Civil War by a Confederate captain. It wasn't a hotel any longer, but a country tenement.

Brandy was four. She envied the people who lived at the old hotel, slapfooted children and adults in makeshift clothes. The height of the balconies thrilled her, the way the tenants could look down on the road with such superior detachment.

Drowsily she smelled iron and rust, and the loaded freight of anthracite and pine, waiting to be hauled. Brandy closed her eyes. She wasn't aware of a man who came down the line and clamped shut the heavy chain that attached the cars to a powerful engine. He tossed a cigarette butt onto the berm and taking off his cap wiped his forehead on his sleeve. September heat made his eyes itch. He climbed aboard and shouted to the engineer.

The engine shuddered and steamed. It strained forward, gathering bulk and tension. Brandy was startled by a tug in the metal frame that encased her. Her eyes widened and her mouth stretched to cry out as the train pulled forward, a shock shuttling down her spine. Her eyes fixed blankly on her blue house. She thought of her mother and father. Instinctively she clutched at the bottom of the car, her ceiling, tearing the skin from her fingers.

Then she felt a hand on her arm, tugging her against the gathering weight of the train—which had moved but a small space, and prepared now to slam ahead—a hand dragging her to safety just as the car snapped forward, striking sparks. A spark bounced off Brandy's cheek, but she didn't feel it. Stunned, she was pulled into daylight. She landed on her backside, her feet sliding into her rescuer's shins.

She blinked. It was a second or two before she looked up to see who it was. She recognized him—Pearly Wainwright.

He rarely spoke, and had the abilities of a child. His hair and skin were paper-white, and his fuzzy ball of hair reminded Brandy of a dandelion gone to seed. His pale blue eyes stared into hers, and he smiled, soft wrinkles forming around his bloodless lips. He still held her hand. Soot had smudged her cheek, but she wasn't injured, except for her scraped fingers.

She moved her flat gaze up and down Pearly Wainwright. He had on soft green trousers and a checked shirt she identified as one her father had given him. Pearly lived at the old hotel. She had waved to him often. In response he did a trick: he lifted his hat, but only the brim would come off. The crown stayed on his head.

They stood holding hands minuet-fashion as the train pumped on down the tracks, steaming farther and farther away on the silver rails until it was gone.

II.

Brandy at sixteen was a cigarette girl at the Virginia State Fair, handing out free packs to men and women and to any teenager who wore lipstick or looked old enough to shave. She'd lied about her age to get the job, saying she was eighteen. Now, in a red-and-white striped jumper and a red cap, she pressed the crisp cardboard packs into outstretched hands too numerous to count. Her mind was fixed on her lover, Bob, foreman of the construction crew that was to tear down the old hotel.

The work had given him access to the building, and he and Brandy made love on a bare mattress in an empty room, after school, before she went off to her job at the fair. She would hang her red-and-white uniform on the doorknob and lie down on the mattress. Of the former tenants, one had just died—a lady named Lila who was old beyond measure—and now only one family remained in the building, occupying several rooms, under a special arrangement with the owner. On warm September evenings, the family—a father, mother, and baby girl—ate their supper outside. Brandy found the scene so poignant as to be almost unbearable: the lush green grass with its late shadows, the plates of food on a card table beneath twisty-limbed oaks, the baby trotting about with a toy in her plump hands. Brandy would speak to the family as she left the old hotel, buttoning the last buttons on her uniform; the family didn't mind that she and Bob had their own secret room on the top floor. Bob slept for a while after they made love. He liked to sleep in late sun, he said, in an empty room.

Brandy felt she was his age, mid-twenties, instead of sixteen. She wanted to get married. Every three or four evenings, she broached the subject to Bob. She dreamed of a yard of her own, a child of her own, and Bob eating supper from a card table set up on the grass. Yet she always pictured her own blue house in the background, where she still lived with her father and mother.

Trains still went by on the tracks just outside the old hotel, but since Brandy had grown up with the sound, it didn't startle her out of love or sleep. In her underwear, scratching at mosquito bites, she stood at the window of the old hotel looking at the passing trains and across the tracks at her blue house.

Her identity with the place was so strong that whenever she imagined escaping, establishing her own independence, she pictured other blue houses, railroad tracks, and old hotels surrounding her. Yet her restlessness invaded every moment. At the fair she admired the young people from the city and from out of town. The fairgrounds were on the east side of

Richmond, sprawling flat acres, half carnival, half agricultural display: the ideal world, Brandy thought, part fun, part work to fuel the fun.

Brandy was enormously sure of herself. She knew where her destiny lay. The construction foreman was her first lover, but she knew she wanted a future with him, a family. Her future was a masterpiece that she carried around in her head. She was small-boned, blonde, nut-brown, with none of the softness and comfort of childbearing in her body. She thought, Why *can't* the wishes of one person actually work out? She was good in math. She applied statistics to happiness. Couldn't just one person find continuous, lifelong delight? And why shouldn't it be herself? The greatest misery, she thought, would be a marriage in which you were only half in love. With Bob, she could be in love forever.

Her parents advised her to wait, to see other men. Brandy set her jaw. She was serious about her schoolwork, studying hard while she had the chance, because college wasn't an option. She felt settled with Bob, and eager to devote her youth to raising her young.

As fall turned colder, the afternoons nippy beneath the polish of sunshine, Bob's orders to raze the old hotel were delayed. He became engrossed with the history of the place. Built in the 1880s, it had lasted so long, he said, that it deserved to keep on surviving. At one time, it was surrounded by manmade lakes, Bob reported, with flocks of peacocks and a herd of tame deer to grace its grounds.

One day he showed Brandy photographs of the original builder—the Confederate captain, a handsome man with shoulder-length dark curls, his fierce face staring down the passage of all those years. The inn had not succeeded; few guests came to drink the waters of its springs. As Bob told

Brandy about this, his face absorbed, she fought the sneaky pangs of jealousy about the dead man and his hotel taking so much of Bob's attention. Lazily she caught a ladybug that had got indoors, and while Bob talked on, she let it crawl up her arm, recalling the old superstition: *She's measuring me for my wedding gloves.*

The current owner of the property died, and all plans to tear it down were suspended. Joyfully, Bob and Brandy got married. He carried her over the threshold of the old hotel and they made love in the room they had come to think of as their own, but they made their home in the blue house where Brandy had lived all her life with her parents. She dreamed of sons and daughters who would play in the woods behind the blue house. She read fairy-tales to Bob as he fell asleep. Six years passed, but they had no children.

III.

Her parents never looked any older. As time went by, they seemed to go backward in age, so that Brandy was the mother and her parents were her siblings and then became her two bright-eyed, straight-mouthed, respectful children, ever neat in their habits and appreciative of what they had. "That was a good chicken we had for supper, yes, a mighty good chicken," her father would murmur, and her mother would say, "This house stays so warm in the winter, so fine and warm," and around Brandy they wore expressions of looking into the distance, and around her husband Bob they stepped lightly, as if around a man asleep.

Much of the time he *was* asleep. Maybe from so much sit-ting and sleeping, his arms grew longer and his trunk shorter, like a chimp, Brandy thought. He sometimes painted houses, but much of the time he was drunk, or just not around. Brandy worked one job after another, at the school cafeteria, as a secretary, a telephone operator, sometimes two jobs at once. She and her mother were never close. They didn't go off together and whisper about the men. They never said anything to each other that Bob or Brandy's father wasn't allowed to hear. They were like distant sisters, disinterested in each other's doings.

At first Brandy used to lay Bob out for not working. She'd yell and threaten and sob and swear, the cords in her thin tough neck standing out. "You used to work so hard," she'd say, and Bob would say, "What a funny little thing I'm married to" and take her in his arms, and they would be happy for a while. Of their barrenness he said, "The world don't need any more people in it," and Brandy would cheer up enough to love him again.

In winter they put on their coats, scrabbled in the hallway closet to find their skates and went to a shallow pond where, when the ice was thick enough, they skated for hours, the blades whining, their laughter a hide-and-seek sound in the falling dusk.

"This is one of *his* lakes," Bob said one night. "The Captain's. There's no natural reason for it to be here. I found it on one of his maps. Notice it's getting smaller, year by year. He built it for his guests to enjoy. They'd row around in those rowboats, with the birds singing and the deer coming up close and the peacocks fanning 'em with their fancy tails."

"You paint a pretty picture," Brandy said. She had heard about the Captain all these years. "Better it were a paycheck."

"He must have had his workers dig the lake," said Bob. "It must've been big, back then. Did he put the fish in it himself, or did they just one day come to be? The fish that live there, are they the descendants of his fish? And what keeps it being a lake at all, instead of the water sinking into the ground, turning into mud, then dust? I come out here at night, Brandy, and pretend I'm him."

Brandy closed her eyes, her feet following the road from memory, the tied skates in her hand banging against her side.

"No reason for the hotel to be condemned all these years, ought to be fixed up nice with you and me running it, it's still in good shape, heart pine like don't hardly grow in the woods anymore . . ." Bob's breath smelled like licorice; the moonlight striking his silver skates made him a tinfoil man.

They reached the railroad tracks. We were the only grown-ups there at the skating pond, thought Brandy, among all those kids. They had to stop for a train to pass, a night train, warm with yellow light, the passengers' heads bent over books, not a one of them seeing the couple who stood there, the woman hearing the word "fifteen" in the thrust and shuttle of the wheels: I'll be fertile for about fifteen more years. I could get myself another man. The train passed by.

"I need some beer," Bob said. They did everything together: she followed him into the squat brick grocery store by the tracks and held his skates while he picked out a couple of sixes. As Brandy paid, Bob told the cashier, "He used to have a deer shelter right here, where this store is. Fed 'em hay and kept 'em like pets. And the peacocks, there got to be so many, it must've been a parade ground for 'em."

The cashier punched the register, made Brandy's change. "You're a regular hiss-torian, Bob," she said, her hard eyes gleaming.

"One time, some idiot took a bow and arrow and shot a little fawn," said Bob, "and the Captain broke down and cried.

I read that in an old newspaper article. The Captain'd been in the war and got shot and seen men die, but still he could cry about a fawn."

"Yep, you showed me your scrapbook," the cashier said. "All I wonder is, if that Captain was so smart, why'd he build his hotel so close to the railroad tracks? Closer than y'all's house, even. No wonder he never had no guests. Who could get a good night's sleep with the train come screaming through the bedroom? You need a bag for the beer?"

Brandy's cheeks burned. He was a drunk and everybody knew it.

She didn't see, she never saw, the depth of his imagination, the part that didn't have to do with drink.

BUT SHE had been in love with only him, and he with her. Bob often said, "We're just like the Captain and his lady. I wish I had a picture of her."

"You've got plenty of *him*," Brandy said, "and too many of Robert E. Lee. That old phony."

"You don't know nothing about Robert E. Lee. He'll come out good in my book."

Brandy knew there would never be a book. Bob just pored over his photographs and scrapbooks. In the last year, he had worked a total of twenty days. He scarcely spoke to Brandy's parents; Brandy felt she inhabited two separate worlds that met only at the table.

One night, Bob came up behind her and placed his hands on her waist. "Do something for me," he said. "Dress up for me and be her, the Captain's lady. Put a long dress on, put your hair up," he whispered, kissing the back of her neck. "Be her."

"I'm sick of those dead people, Bob. I'm not her and you're not him. Leave me alone." It was late and Brandy was tired.

Her parents were asleep. She gathered the beer cans Bob had lined up on the mantelpiece.

Bob grabbed her arm. "What good's a wife who won't share her husband's hobby?"

"It's not a hobby anymore, it's something strange." She found a can of beer that was nearly full, and she leaned her head back and drank it down. Defiantly, she stared at him—she, who never drank.

He snatched the can from her hand and threw it to the floor. His hair was in his eyes and he looked old, older than her father. She cried out, and he pulled her toward the door. Coatless, they went out into the ringing December evening, and he made her get into the car.

They sped through the silent streets of the village and then took the highway into Richmond. All Bob said was, "You'll see where I visit him."

"I don't want to," Brandy said.

She rubbed her cold hands together. It was past midnight, and the city streets were empty. Slums and fine houses flashed past her window; in the distance the lights of the warehouse district sparkled down by the river. Brandy's stomach churned from the beer. She could still taste its bitterness on her tongue.

Bob drove fast to Cherry Street, entering Hollywood Cemetery through its heavy iron gates, which were wide open as if this were the middle of the day. It was dark and the streets of the necropolis were narrow, and Bob drove roughly, so the tires of the car squeezed against the curb. They sped from the base of the hill to the top, round and round, so Brandy was dizzy, sick, begging him to stop. She rolled down her window, and cold air stung her skin. The headlights caught in their glare the ornate monuments and headstones.

"Now they are dust," said Bob. He accelerated, then reversed, the car rocking and bumping as they wound upwards to a bluff, then down, through the thousands of dead. Bob said, "I know everybody here," and he laughed. At last he stopped the car. Brandy's head whirled. He came around to her side and pulled her out. "Look, there they rest, the Captain and his lady."

Her knees buckling, she saw two big stones. She read the names. Bob was reciting the inscriptions as if in prayer. Brandy's fingers and toes were numb. Moonlight picked out the markers all around them—so many she could never count them all, more dead people than there were stars, frosted and colder than cold.

"And Jeff Davis, he's up here too," said Bob. He tugged at Brandy's hand. She jerked away from him and sprang back into the car, fumbling for the keys, starting it up, accelerating with the door still open and scraping against the low curb. Bob yelled but she took off, the car lurching as she twisted along the cramped streets, each one a serpentine journey between the graves, each one a sly ruse to keep her lost. She reached what she thought was the entrance, but it was a circular drive around a mausoleum like a tiny castle; the headlights exposed an altar with a vase of dried frozen flowers, and then she bounced up against the curb and the engine stalled and she hit the steering wheel hard, honking the horn with her ribs, bruising them.

In the silence that followed, she heard Bob yelling her name. She pushed open the door, climbed out, and strained for balance. She heard him coming closer, though she couldn't see him among the thousand stones. She crept away from the car, her limbs so chilled she couldn't feel them, her fingertips cold as the earth, and knelt behind a marble obelisk topped with a cluster of marble grapes. A big barberry bush grew there, and she crept beneath it for shelter. She wanted to be as dark as the darkness, yet she felt him finding her, heard him coming nearer, his footsteps nimble among the plots. She put her hands up over her head, scratching her fingers on the thorns. Bob's voice bounced and echoed, loud as thunder among the stones, loud as a locomotive, and she opened her mouth and screamed.

Having never told her parents or anyone else about the incident when she was four, she had forgotten it until her husband stood above her and a light snow began to fall, dusting the stones with fine crystals, powdering Bob's hair as he scowled down at her. She crawled out from beneath the barberry bush and stood up.

"Jesus, let's go home," Bob said. "It's better in the daylight anyway."

"Pearly Wainwright," she said.

"Why, no, I haven't thought about him in years," her mother said.

"Not since I gave him some clothes," her father said, "a few shirts, a pair of shoes, an old coat torn but still warm. He wore it inside the old hotel, he told me. All's they had for heat was fireplaces."

"Old Pearly?" said the cashier at the grocery store. "Well, I guess he wadn't so old, he just never seemed young. He been gone for years and years."

"He's still 'round here," an old man told Brandy. "I seen him just t'other day, you mean the short dark fellow works on cars?"

"No," said Brandy. "He was tall—and pale . . ."

An old black woman told her, "I remember tendin' him when he was sick, and when I went back to check on 'im, his room was empty and t'others say he dead."

"Pearly Wainwright," said Bob, twirling his glass so the beer foamed up the sides. "I've lived around here all my life and never heard of any such person."

"He saved me," Brandy said. "It's important for me to thank him. More important, even, than having a child."

Brandy was too tired to talk. In the week since her recollection, she had spent all her time asking people about her savior. She had knocked on doors of houses so old she had almost forgotten they existed behind their screens of trees. She had called *hello* into cabins deep in the woods. She had interviewed her old teachers, retired now in their peeling Victorian houses on the four good streets of the village. She stared into the fire and thought about him. Pearly.

"Wain . . ." sighed Bob, falling asleep.

She gazed into the flames, remembering. When had she seen him last? An image formed in her mind: Pearly Wainwright walking up the railroad tracks, early spring, a day with clouds like blue spider webs and the sharp scent of wild onions in the air. Pearly wore a long black coat. His pale fizzy hair caught the light. He walked stiff, taking his hands out of his pockets and putting them in again. He walked far down and then round the bend to the vanishing point. Brandy grew convinced she was the last person, in those parts, to see him. Walking along the tracks. How else would a person leave this place? He never glanced back.

Why thank him for this life? But she kept on looking.

SHE FOUND him in Ashland, the next town north. She drove there on a Sunday, while her parents were in church and Bob got ready to drink the day away, pouring beer from one glass into another and back again. She drove on the narrow flat road to the next town, stopped at the soda fountain, and asked the old men at the counter, eating ham and okra and cobbler, "Do any of you know Pearly Wainwright?"

The old men jingled change in their pockets, a waiting sound, tense. Their silence told her she was close.

"What he look like?" said a voice.

"Tall and pale," she said, "different."

"Like how?" said the voice. It belonged to a man ferociously wrinkled, his skin a paper bag crunched up in a million lines. "What he do with a hat?"

"A hat," she said. "Yes, a hat. He lifts off the brim but the crown stays on his head."

"You got a sewing machine, miss?" a bald man said, and the others shushed him.

"That hat trick, that's him all right," said the wrinkled man. He sighed. "Take that road that goes out of town. Turn off when you see a little swamp."

"You got a sewing machine?" the bald man barked, and the others laughed.

"A sewing machine?" Brandy said.

"Never mind," said the wrinkled man. "More coffee," he told the waitress. "Don't you know I like m'cup full?"

She wondered as she drove why all her life she'd been on old roads, in spite of the new ones all around, the ones people talked about. She made the turn at the swamp. A big dead cypress stared down at its reflection in shallow black water. Buzzards hunkered in the branches. The road curved away into sand, past a stand of pines. The only house she saw was three stories tall, once grand, now painted pink like fresh sunburn. Smoke from the chimney spun lazy as a slow-moving rope.

A woman answered her knock.

"Pearly," Brandy said. "Pearly Wainwright. Are you Mrs. Wainwright?"

The woman wasn't young or old. She twittered over her shoulder to someone else. Another woman appeared at her side. They were dressed alike, in plaid shirtwaists with aprons. Their eyes were avid in the pupil. They wore their hair in braids crossed over their heads. The hair was mostly brown, shot through with silver. The second woman spoke in a language Brandy didn't know.

"Pearly Wainwright," she repeated, and they motioned her inside.

The living room had windows from floor to ceiling, all cracked, a branch of a spruce tree poking through one pane. The furniture was hidden beneath mounds of cloth. In the middle of the room sat two sewing machines, old-fashioned and black, giving off a faint sweet scent of motor oil.

Then she saw him, silhouetted in a doorway across the room, the light behind him making his fuzzy hair shine, his hands in his pockets, his head bent in the angle of someone smiling at a child. He came to her with his hands outstretched, and she let him take her hands in his, while she searched his pale empty eyes.

She meant to say, "I'm Brandy. Thank you." But what she said instead was, "Why did you leave?"

His white lips moved. The two aproned women settled themselves at their sewing machines and commenced to operate the treadles. Busily they folded the cloth and stitched and pushed it past the bright flashing needles.

"Why did you leave home?" Brandy said. She named the village.

Pearly Wainwright smiled. He had not grown older. The sewing machines sang *glip glip glip*. Pearly said, "I got tired of the train."

Brandy leaned forward to catch his words. She said, "You saved my life. When I was little, I hid beneath the train. You pulled me out. I want to say thank you."

Glip glip glip, the sewing machines hummed. Pearly looked at her as if waiting for her to leave. "I don't remember," he said. He shook his pale head from side to side.

"Lots of people remember *you*," Brandy said. "My parents, and the cashier at the grocery store, and the woman who tended you one year when you were sick."

He listened politely, the smile still fixed on his lips. She mentioned the names of others, but he only shook his head. Brandy heard herself grow impatient. She said, "Don't you want to know what happened to everybody? I got married. My husband's name is Bob. He used to work on the old hotel. It's still standing there, right across the tracks from my house."

"I expect it'll be torn down some day," said Pearly. He rocked back and forth, his hands in his pockets, and she waited for more, but that was all he said.

The spruce branches scratched the windowpanes. The sunlight on the old walls was so bright it hurt her eyes. Her memories were clearer than the man in front of her—Pearly waving from the porch of the old hotel, with his trick hat; Pearly pulling her out from under the train. She could hear the screech of the freight cars and smell the soot and oil—but it was just the oil from the sewing machines. Cold air flowed through the broken window and swirled around her ankles.

"Good-bye, then," she said. The two women looked up, their eyes four blue marbles. She clenched her teeth. She wouldn't cry. On her way out, she saw Pearly's trick hat in two pieces hanging on pegs by the door—the crown, the brim. From an umbrella stand, a bunch of peacock feathers stared at her with their thousand eyes. She found the knob with her cold fingers. *Glip glip,* the machines said.

"MAYBE HE saved them too," Bob said. "If you took him a sewing machine, he'd let you stay. Maybe he finds all his women under trains. Can't blame a man for having two women if he can get 'em." He rolled over and began to snore.

Brandy dreamed of jumping on the train, her feet jerking in sleep. She felt the heavy motion in her arms as she clutched the ladder of a car, her body bending in the wind like a blade. Then she was with the Captain. He rowed her out to the middle of his crystal lake, and from the shore his tame deer swam out to meet them. His voice sounded just like Bob's. "He didn't remember *saving your life?*" he said, and he laughed and laughed, but the sound was lost in the roar of the rushing engine and the singing rails.

Syrup and Feather

JULIA RESIGNED HER teaching job in February because she was getting married. She needed time to make her gown and trousseau for the April wedding. Embroidering daisies on fingertip towels, she had never been so happy or so alone, her future a bright blank stretch of security. She sewed all day in her rented room in Glen Allen, having taught school for less than two years. She liked teaching but didn't love it. She did enjoy being sixty miles away from her home in Toano, over in James City County, where her widowed mother ran a small inn.

In 1917, it was expected that young female teachers in rural Virginia would marry and leave, even in the middle of a term.

Julia's fiancé, a doctor from Tennessee, lived in Richmond. They had met when he visited relatives in Toano. They became engaged at Christmastime, and when she returned to school in the New Year, her students, all different ages, clustered around the diamond ring on her hand. She let them try it on.

She'd never heard anybody talk about the kind of joy she felt in these sewing days, the only sounds the birds' calls and the whisper of thread through cloth. She fell into reverie, winding ribbon around her fingers as if it were a daughter's hair. She wrote to Edgar, her fiancé, but she did not really want to see him in those weeks leading up to the wedding. Richmond was only nine miles away, but she told him not to come, she was busy. She wrote instead, describing the lace she was stitching onto pillowcases and the tiny imitation pearls on her veil.

They were married in Richmond at the home of a prominent surgeon, Edgar's mentor. There was no money for a honeymoon. Immediately after the wedding and after seeing Julia's mother off to Toano on the train, they went to the house that Edgar had found for them.

The house was terrifying to Julia. Edgar had bought it by paying the back taxes. It was a crumbling mansion in a forgotten part of Richmond, vacant since the death of its former occupant, a Mrs. Mabry, twenty years earlier. Plates were still laid out on a cobwebbed table—fine porcelain plates, yellowed from well water and crazed with cracks. Somehow the house had escaped vandals, except for thefts of most of its furniture and one mantel. A railroad switching yard adjoined the property. Day and night, trains emitted grinding, teeth-rattling clashes. Julia hated the noise and the fact that the house had no indoor plumbing. She had never had that luxury before, and now that she was married, she had thought— but she didn't say that.

"We won't be here long, I promise you," Edgar said. He gazed at the fence that was their only protection from the switching yard. "Anybody could climb over that. Maybe I've done a stupid thing. Look, I'll put my revolver here, on the mantel. If you need it, use it."

He had an affinity for railways, having worked as a telegraph operator for the East Tennessee and Western North Carolina Railroad while he saved money for medical school. He grew up poor, as she had. He couldn't afford medical school until he was over thirty, and now there were debts to be paid.

Edgar hired a carpenter and a painter, and there was a woman, Dessie, to help Julia. Dessie said she had known old Mrs. Mabry, who lived in the house for so long. Dessie explained the plates in the dining room. "After her funeral, I washed these plates myself," she said. "When she didn't have no family to take them away, I just put them back on the table."

"YOUR HUSBAND has the most brilliant medical mind I've ever encountered," the head surgeon told Julia, at a lavish dinner in the best part of town. The house had fine furniture but little of it, for the host, like Edgar, was a young doctor just starting out. The elegant rooms were cold. Julia was cold, though her dress was more modest than those of the other wives, whose shoulders were bare.

"Your husband has developed new techniques for the eye and ear," the surgeon went on. "He'll get offers to move to other cities. I want to keep him here. You'll help me, won't you?" His silvery, whiskery smile scared her.

"Yes, sir," she said.

"I worry about that house you're in," the man said. "A good address makes a difference. Why, out where you are now, you'll miss all the fun with the other gals—the garden club meetings, the luncheons."

"It's all right," Julia said. Her mother always said she was stubborn. "I like that house," and as she said it, it became true.

Edgar was away all day, from first light till well after dark. He didn't know that with the warm spring weather came a parade of travelers, hoboes riding the rails and wandering through the switching yard to the house. The first time it happened, Dessie came to Julia and said a man was wanting food.

"You feed one, be feeding them all," said Dessie.

"Give him part of that roast hen and some bread," Julia directed her.

A cavalcade of tramps began, old and young. She never saw them climb the fence. She just heard the knocks on the kitchen door, light taps or hard rapping like a woodpecker drilling for bugs. She took to preparing meals as soon as Edgar was out of the house. Water was always available for the men, with a dipper hanging by the well. The water was cold as melted snow.

Dessie got into the spirit of it. "Why don't I fry up a big mess of sausage," she'd say, "so we can make sausage biscuits."

Julia had known itinerant tinkers and bums while growing up and working at the Hotel Felix, the little inn that her parents ran in the house where Julia had grown up. She'd hated living among the guests and boarders, hated the work of the inn, the endless scrubbing and fetching, the slop jars and chamber pots she had to empty. Always in her memory, she was cleaning up some rank mess a guest had made, and her father was sick, then dying. When tramps came by, her mother, an accomplished cook whose pie crust was cut in tiny pieces to be used by the church for communion every Sunday, fed them sternly. "They're nothing to fool with," her mother said.

Yet Julia, one month married, enjoyed the procession of travelers who came to what she thought of as Mrs. Mabry's house. They were black and white, and a few were foreign. Most were eager to work in exchange for food. She got a flowerbed put in, and a vegetable garden.

Edgar noticed the gardens and said, "Oh, you had the men do that," believing the work was done by his hired men, whom Julia had dismissed. Was it bad not to tell him the truth?

A silent man with a hunched-up shoulder fixed the back steps. A boy was with him. With his low cap and baggy pants, the boy might be a girl in disguise. Julia put extra food into those outstretched, dainty, dirty hands: a ripe pear, fried pie, drumstick, cornbread sweet with butter.

Hot weather came, and Julia squeezed lemons for lemonade. A very old man gulped his portion and closed his eyes as if he were dying right there in her backyard, under Julia's white sheets flapping on the clothesline in the hot wind. What if he did die? What would she tell Edgar? When he opened his eyes, he talked about the Civil War, about being wounded and being brought on a stretcher to this very house. A shade tree covered the old man and Julia in darkness, though it was afternoon.

Edgar was very late that night. Julia sent Dessie home and sat outside waiting for him. Finally, Edgar drove up in the buggy, swung down from the seat, and caught her around the waist. She smelled cigar smoke and tasted whiskey as he kissed her. He took off his fine leather shoes and left them on the porch, saying they were dirty.

"I go to boxing matches sometimes. Downtown." He hesitated. "I lost money tonight."

He led her to the bedroom. She would have a chicken coop put in, and Dessie could sell the eggs for her. It never hurt to have egg money, even when you were a doctor's wife.

"Dɪᴅ ᴛʜᴇ tramps come by when Mrs. Mabry was here?" Julia asked Dessie.

"She let them sleep in her yard sometimes, but she didn't feed them. The word out on you, though. Some mark over your door by now." Dessie's hands slapping dough were lively.

"How old are you, Dessie?" Julia wondered if Dessie as a girl had really washed those funeral plates.

"Thirty-four."

Older than Julia, by many years. Julia said, "I was brought up not to speak to strangers. I wonder what I'm doing now." Why did she think just then of her mother's pie crust, delicately baked for communion wafers, cut and laid in a stiff linen napkin?

"They won't come by in the evening," Dessie said. "They don't want to shame you."

Jᴜʟɪᴀ ʜᴀᴅ a letter from a girlhood friend who had also been a teacher—for only one year, as compared with Julia's one and a half—and also had married. "You would not guess where I am living now," the letter ran. "On St. Mary's Bay in Nova Scotia. Up on a hill. It's always foggy. I miss Toano, don't you Julia? I live in the clouds," and the last words were underlined.

Julia sat with pen and paper in hand, thinking she could tell her friend about the hoboes—all the stories she didn't tell Edgar. She could describe the food that she and Dessie made for them. She could ask her friend why Edgar didn't notice how much money was being spent on meat, flour, sugar, and coffee. She could write that the revolver was still on the mantel where Edgar laid it that first day. Had Edgar really thought she would use a gun or need one?

But all that would take so long to tell, so she wrote her other news, news she hadn't told Edgar yet, about expecting a baby. *Remember how the mothers back home used to keep a baby happy,* she wrote. *They put a drop of syrup on the baby's hand and gave it a feather, and the baby passed the feather back and forth from one sticky little hand to the other.*

THE HEAD surgeon's wife took her to her own dressmaker, saying, "You're not showing yet. You have some time. Oh," and she waved her hand, "I know you sew your own clothes, but this woman is from France. From Paris."

The downtown shop smelled of gardenias. Trilling and clucking, the Frenchwoman set a costly hat on Julia's head as if placing a dome over an iced cake, careful not to smudge the frosting, and said, "There. *Oui.*"

Out on the street, the surgeon's wife said, "You've never seen your husband's office? You haven't met Maida, his secretary? Come on," and Julia, hatbox under her arm, was tugged along.

"If there's any man living who can help the blind to see, it's your husband," said Maida, the secretary, who with her red hair and green eyes was fiercely beautiful, and who spoke in a strange rhythm. She sat at an oak desk, writing down the names of patients, fetching files, and answering the telephone.

"Maida is Welsh," said the surgeon's wife, beaming, "thus her cute accent. My husband found her for Edgar, Julia. She can take dictation faster than anyone you've ever seen, and how she can type! Oh, and this is Gertrude Smith, Edgar's nurse."

A rawboned creature in a white uniform galloped by, a slash of pink scalp showing through her hair. Gertrude Smith nodded to Julia and lumbered down the hallway to Edgar's examining room. "He's with a patient," Gertrude called over her shoulder.

In the elevator, as they left the medical arts building, the surgeon's wife said, "It's so funny about Gertrude Smith.

Everybody always calls her by both names. Gertrude Smith. Poor soul! So clumsy and unattractive. What's the matter, Julia?"

Julia was silent. Her stomach plunged sickeningly as the elevator descended.

"My dear, you will just have to trust your husband. Maida, too," said the older woman.

"I hate her," Julia said, and the tears flowed.

The woman patted her arm. "If you knew more about Maida, you wouldn't hate her. She came to this country on a coal boat. She almost starved to death over there."

Maida had a ring which Edgar bought and gave to Julia, a cloudy emerald which he explained had been in Maida's family for a long time. "I bought it as a way to give her some money," he said, "and it's something pretty for you."

Green as Maida's eyes. Weren't they supposed to be saving, not spending? Julia slipped the ring off her finger and put it in a drawer, and Edgar didn't ask about it.

SHE COULD tell when someone was waiting at the door, could hear the lifting of a hand, the swallow of a dry throat. She never let the men come inside, and they never asked. These calls had rules, formal protocol. Sometimes she checked, to make sure she wasn't going crazy. The other doctors' wives talked about that. Going crazy was fashionable. But she was only handing food and drink out the door, getting her scissors sharpened and her shoes resoled. By the hottest part of summer, she'd seen some of the faces more than once.

She found a chunk of pink quartz beside her back door. It was like stumbling upon a fallen star. There was a picture frame made of twigs, a little deer carved from cherry wood, a fistful of roses in a chipped vase: stolen from whose house, or found by whose hand? She was the hoboes' sweetheart, the queen of tramps. The train brought the men and took them away, the way critters carried burrs on their fur.

She had Dessie mend their shirts and pants.

"Some of 'em running from the law," Dessie said, sewing.

"We don't know which ones," Julia said, "and maybe they didn't do anything wrong."

Edgar caught a summer cold and stayed at home. He fretted in bed while she rushed to him with soup and fanned his face. All day, no knocks on the door, no tired feet in the yard. Did a mark over her door say he was home? She looked, but she couldn't find it.

In winter, news came from far away, from Tennessee, a telegram with word of sickness in Edgar's family, and he went to them. They lived up on a mountain. Julia stayed behind, trying to picture the place, the faces. She had never met any of her husband's Tennessee relatives.

She hadn't intended to give a party. She and Dessie had been baking apple pies all day, for it was cold, and then the men showed up, two and three, bringing meat and onions for stew. She had Dessie haul out Mrs. Mabry's biggest pot from the cellar and scrub it, and the men cooked over a fire in the yard. She and Dessie fried a chicken. The music started at sundown, harmonicas, Jew's harps, a fiddle or two. She went outside and passed the chicken and apple pies around. The men ate from the metal pans, cupping their hands to catch the crumbs and apple slices. A man had died on the rails that day, jumping from a fast train and breaking his neck. "Here's to One-Eye Slim," the men said, and raised their tin cups.

When the baby came, she would stop all this.

GERTRUDE SMITH told her about the trip to Tennessee, for Edgar had told Gertrude about it: how he walked through deep snow up the mountainside and performed a tracheotomy on his niece on the kitchen table. "Diphtheria. She would have died," Gertrude Smith said. "By the time he was down the mountain again, his feet were frozen." Gertrude rummaged in a cabinet for a bottle. "Make him pour this on his feet every night," she said. Upon his return, he had gone directly from the train station to his office, sending word to Julia to bring him fresh clothes.

Maida, at her desk, twittered like a fancy bird. "How are you feeling?" she said, meaning the baby.

"Fine," Julia said. She'd had another letter from her friend in Canada, in the fog, saying: *If I'd known how little I would see the sun, I would not have come here.*

Three nuns stepped into the waiting room, and Maida jumped to her feet to greet them. Julia recalled what Edgar said of them: bad eyesight from the poor light in the convent, and their headdresses shut the light out even more.

"I'll take these to him," said Gertrude Smith, reaching for the clothes Julia had brought.

That night, Edgar told Julia he had gambling debts. "I've stopped going to boxing matches," he said, "but I've got to pay what I owe."

She gave him the egg money, and the next day she took Maida's ring to a jeweler, sold it, and gave him that money, too. It wasn't enough. But she was glad, because it meant they would stay in Mrs. Mabry's house a while longer.

Edgar put the money in his pocket and said, "Maida had me take her to a match one night. I didn't think she should go. She'd say, 'O ho!' every time a man hit the floor."

"You spent the evening with her?"

"Don't ever think it was any more than that." He looked so taken aback that she believed him.

SHE THOUGHT about her students as she cooked, pouring butter over a chicken so that the skin would brown. She used to point to countries on a map, making mistakes, saying, "No, that's not right." Once, a rich woman asked Julia to bring the pupils to pick daffodils on her farm. Julia declared a holiday and worked for the same wage her students earned. How glorious that day was, picking armloads of flowers till sundown. The rich woman said the flowers would go to florists all over the East Coast.

She shouldn't have done that, trading a school day for a day of daffodils. She should have helped her pupils form ambitions, something beyond the plow. The chalkboard in that schoolhouse was a piece of linoleum painted black. Her precious sticks of chalk wore out fast. The girls made her a buttercup quilt as a wedding present. And the boys! They wore black armbands on her last day, to mourn her leaving. That was the funniest thing.

Melted butter on the chicken; herbs in the cavity for a savory smell as it roasted in the stove. She enjoyed cooking, and she and Dessie taught each other recipes. As she leaned down to put the chicken in the oven, pain tore through her middle, and she dropped the pan with a cry.

I felt my baby die. Weeks later, she wrote that one sentence to her friend in Canada. The whole time that her mother was there, tending her during her long recovery, none of the tramps came by. Only when her mother left did they start up again.

"Lady, every hobo from here to California knows you lost a baby," a man told her at the door, accepting a sandwich, "and we are sorry, ma'am."

She was still shaky. Dessie draped a shawl around her shoulders and said, "You got to come in now," and Julia did.

Some shadow passed over her. "What did Mrs. Mabry die from?" she asked Dessie.

"She was old. Must have been ninety, ninety-five."

"Nobody came in and got her? Killed her?"

"Why do you say that?" Dessie said.

"Because nobody moved in after she died. Because anybody could run through here, anybody. That's what my husband said."

"Do you want to make them stop coming?"

"No," Julia said, "I don't want that." The bad feeling lifted. She could fry some potatoes, and wasn't there some gingerbread left over that wouldn't be missed if she halved it, halved it again, and gave away what she sliced thin?

She didn't want to go with the railriders, just wanted what they brought her—her best self giving, giving to them of all she had. They were quieter than animals. She pictured animals in the night with glowing eyes, footfalls and pawfalls.

"Dessie, where's your house?" she asked.

"Out there," and Dessie gestured, smiling as if to mean, what? That there was no house, no place she went?

MORE AND more, Julia thought about the operation Edgar had done on his niece, a little girl on a kitchen table, with deep snow outside the house.

"What did you give her, beforehand, so she wouldn't feel the pain?" she asked.

"Ether," he answered.

So she added ether to the scene, and she got out of him that it was past midnight when he operated, the room lit with all the lanterns the family could find.

"What had they eaten for supper?"

"I don't know," he said, tired, from his side of the bed.

She wanted what that niece had had—to fall asleep and wake healing, knowing there were years ahead of her, enough time to go back to sleep, for now.

"ARE THERE others like me?" she asked a man, thinking she should start counting them, keep some record of their faces, voices, habits.

"There's a lady in Wisconsin who gives us real fine cheese," the man said. "A woman in Missouri took a bullet out of my leg."

"And how are they not like me?"

"You will miss us, when you're gone." He tore into his food, never mind his broken teeth.

CUSTARD WITH a crust of sugar, vanilla, and nutmeg, baked in glass dishes etched with designs of flowers. Chilled tomato aspic, just this side of icy, topped with lemon slices. White meat of chicken cooked, sliced, pressed into a round mold with gelatin and crushed almonds, garnished with green grapes and homemade mayonnaise: supper party food, charming and delicious. People talked about the war at these gatherings, but the war barely touched her. She was figuring out the recipes for the food she tasted.

She had married above herself, for Edgar was brilliant, but like her, he was country. For him, she cooked white beans with ham hocks, a dish he'd carried in his heart from East Tennessee.

The second summer came, the second summer at Mrs. Mabry's house. Wind blew all night, a ceaseless breeze from the world's four corners. She pictured a beach she had visited as a child, with long rollers sweeping in. You could play in the water before a hurricane came. She was well from the baby, but she couldn't sleep. At night, she saw the lights of the city through the tossing trees. She imagined grandchildren, widowhood: potted begonias, a pantry smelling of cinnamon and mace and chocolate, and a trunk that held her wedding dress, the buttercup quilt, and the block of pink quartz.

"I want to meet your niece," she told Edgar. "Let's send her a train ticket and have her up for a visit."

He nodded and wiped his mustache with a napkin, but he didn't send a ticket. Would the girl have a hole in her throat, a bloody line across her neck? The child was so far away, ever in snow, sitting up on the kitchen table and swinging her feet over the edge, breathing again and asking for something to eat. That was how it was in the Bible, the damsel not dead but sleeping.

THE DAY of daffodil picking was not her only dereliction as a teacher. Sometimes she took her students out into the woods so they could teach her the names of wildflowers. "That's ninebark," they announced, swinging through the forest. "There's mullein, gayfeather, fairy cup." The children danced ahead of her. They found Indian pipe, wake-robin, frostflower, boneset, queen of the meadow, stargrass, and touch-me-not. "I know this one," Julia said, pointing out hens-and-chickens. "My mother grows that."

Another time, when she had used up all her lessons for the day—penmanship and reading, spelling and hygiene—she took them outside for games. They played blind man's bluff and antnyover until they were breathless.

She might get pregnant again and have her first child at Mrs. Mabry's house, and then she and Edgar and the baby would move to a new house with a green tiled roof and a brick garage opening onto a cool, leafy alley. One day soon, Edgar would come home and say he had found that house. What if she refused to go? She could get by on very little. She could sew for a living. She missed her students, their faces dime-bright, their presence like dimes come alive. When they got wild, she used to tease them, saying, *Running away with yourselves.*

"It's quite wonderful here, Julia. I see why you like this house," said the surgeon's wife, balancing a teacup on her knee. "Don't be in a hurry to leave, no matter what my husband says."

This woman always saw more than Julia thought she would.

"Did you know Mrs. Mabry?" Julia asked.

"I'm not sure there ever *was* a Mrs. Mabry. Oh, you hear things. The Yankees used this house as their headquarters, didn't they, camped and had a hospital here. I've seen the old photographs of sick men in the yard. Why, that great big tree out there, they lay under it."

"But she wasn't real—Mrs. Mabry? Dessie knew her. Dessie washed the plates when she died. It's her day off. If she were here, she could tell you about that."

As if alive, the teacup jumped on the woman's knee. She shook her head, dismissing all this talk. "Julia," she said. "I've got to tell you something important, something about your husband. It's not Maida, it's never been Maida. It's Gertrude Smith."

Gertrude Smith. The galloping rawbones. "How do you know this?"

"It won't be so bad for you," said the surgeon's wife, rising from her chair, "if you can just let them be."

"I don't believe it." Gertrude Smith taking the fresh clothes from her, clumping down the hallway with a basin in her hands to catch blood—yes, Julia did believe it. "Why tell me this?"

The surgeon's wife walked to the window, pushed the curtain aside, and said, "He couldn't marry anybody like that. He married *you*. If I were you, I'd try not to think about it. Ah, look. You can see the river from here, the James, just a glimmer." She let the curtain fall, set her cup and saucer on the mantel, and gave a small shriek. "Do you know you've got a gun here, Julia? Don't shoot me!" and she made a wild, comical face.

"O ho," said Julia. Wasn't that what Edgar said Maida said, at the boxing match: *O ho!*

Julia wanted to shoot her. She could kill this woman and get away with it, this person smoothing her elaborate dress and expressing thanks for the tea. The tramps would take the blame for her. Any one of them would gently remove the gun from Julia's hand, nudge his patched shoe against the body of the surgeon's wife, and advise, "Tell the law that *I* done it, ma'am. Say that she was bein' a nuisance to you, an' I shot her. I'll be on my way now. They'll never find me."

The thought made her laugh, first a chuckle, then a guffaw. The surgeon's wife asked, "What is it? What's so funny?"

Oh, she hadn't laughed in so long, and it felt so good. Howls of laughter started deep in her lungs and bubbled up to her throat. The surgeon's wife said a hasty good-bye and let herself out. Julia couldn't wait for Edgar to come home so she could tell him about the tramps, all of it, even the fact that she had failed to love him.

She washed the teacups and paced the floor. There was no reason to keep secrets any longer. Stay with him or not? She changed her mind a hundred times before he walked through the door.

SHE TOLD the story of the busybody and the gun, oh, a version of it, to her children when they were young enough to laugh just because she herself was laughing. And she told them about Dessie, how she and Dessie had cooked good food for friends of theirs, men who rode on trains.

"What happened to Dessie?" the children asked, and Julia always said she needed to find out, she missed her.

Jane's Hat

BACK WHEN STOCKING caps were in fashion, those long knit caps of bright yarn with tassels on the end, back when my friend Jane had the best stocking cap in school, Mr. Overton Underhill came biking up behind us and snatched Jane's cap right off her head.

It was February 1968. Just that afternoon, Mr. Underhill, who was the principal, had lectured our class on earthquakes. "The ground opens up in a sneer," he had said, and thus I had learned the word *sneer.*

And now he had stolen Jane's hat.

"Ha!" he said and pedaled away with it, his face—with its stubbly cheeks and eyebrows like check marks—swiveling back to gloat at us, the cap rippling in his grasp.

Jane and I were on bikes, too, and we gave chase, pumping our legs hard as we could, keeping him in sight, once getting near enough to see that one of his shoes was untied. He was too burly for his bike, but he was so fast. Sweet wind blew through the broom sedge on either side of the road, and the overarching trees were rusty with winter. Yet it was a warm, fine day.

He beat us to the railroad tracks, where a train came by. It was such a long, long train. Jane and I stood straddling our bikes in its smoky breeze, and when it was past, we rolled across the tracks, but he was gone. He wasn't at the grocery store or the post office or on the porch of the old hotel—the public parts of Glen Allen—or if he were, he'd hidden the bike and gone inside. He must have been far down Mountain Road by then, or off on one of the side roads that still felt like country.

"Where's your hat, Jane?" her mother asked when we burst into her house.

"Mr. Underhill's got it," Jane said, but her mother wasn't listening. She was fitting a cowgirl dress on Jane's sister Tammy.

"Where's my boots?" Tammy demanded.

"Mr. Underhill's got 'em," I said, and we all laughed, even Jane's mother with her mouth full of pins. Tammy giggled, but carefully because of her lipstick. In my mind I heard what Mama always said about Tammy: *Five years old and lipstick on, and the way she dances.*

Jane never did get her hat back. From then on, whenever we couldn't find something, we'd say, "Mr. Underhill's got it!"

But hadn't he given us something, too—the beautiful chase with the sweet wind and the trees overhead and only the three of us on that empty road almost too narrow for two cars to pass? The intervening train was only fate, and the world was about to change anyway, so why worry about a hat?

"Have you ever seen a blackbird fly with a dove?" Mr. Underhill asked everybody, in assembly, the day after he stole Jane's stocking cap. "No, and you never will. Still, we must accept the decisions the government makes for us, however misguided."

I thought of the earthquake lecture, how he had interrupted Miss Stancil in the middle of her math lesson to deliver the information about the earth opening up like a sneer. "I must ask you to make them welcome," he said, turning to address the teachers, who sat very straight in the aisle seats of the auditorium as he strode back and forth on the stage, "but I don't ask you to fly with them."

The blackbirds would not come in a flock, just a few at a time, we learned: a trial period. There would be a girl, Dorothy, in the sixth grade, and her brother, Herman, in Miss Stancil's fifth-grade class—Jane's and my class.

Mr. Underhill said, "Any questions?"

How vast the silence was, with a hundred children and six teachers thinking about blackbirds and doves. I stood up and said, "What about Jane's stocking cap?"

But the instant I spoke, the bell rang, just as the train had hurtled between Mr. Underhill and Jane and me on our bikes, twenty-three hours earlier. So nobody heard me. They just got up and shuffled out the double doors at the rear of the auditorium.

Back in the classroom, Miss Stancil announced that she had intended to give us a quiz on earthquakes. "But I forgot to write it up!" she said.

Jane laughed, with Miss Stancil joining in. So did everybody but me. I felt vaguely disappointed, for I loved mimeographs, if not quizzes: purple sheets of paper with that chemical scent. No quiz. And it was time to go home.

But I was marking time by the theft of Jane's hat. I had loved it, the knotty, holly-green expanse of it and the ball of yellow fringe on the end.

It had smelled of Jane's mother's perfume, ancient precious stuff from France that smelled like cider and roses, the perfume that Tammy wore for her Little Miss Virginia pageant rehearsals—where who would preside as chief judge but Mr. Overton Underhill? Tammy was doused with the fabulous perfume, whereas Jane and I had to steal it, drop by drop.

The day of not-flying-with-blackbirds wasn't over, not even after the assembly and the canceled quiz. As Jane and I set out on our bikes, we encountered Mr. Underhill again, but this time he was on foot, beside the chain link fence of the playground, on the path we sometimes took through the woods—the alternate way to Jane's house. The previous day, he had addressed us both, or maybe just Jane, with the one word, the syllable, "Ha!"

There on the path, he raised his palm and spoke only to me, as if we'd been talking for a long time. "Laurie," he said, "don't ever let anybody know *how* easy it is for you."

"What's easy for you?" asked Jane, as we hurtled pell-mell through the woods, leaving him behind. "Math?" she said. "What did he mean?"

My mouth opened, and the answer came out: "Forgiveness."

Jane stopped her bike so fast she fell off it. "What?"

And I said it again.

"I DON'T remember that," Jane says of the stolen hat, as we eat bistro fare at a restaurant in downtown Richmond, a restaurant that used to be a train station. Its great round clock still hangs on the wall. The ticket counter is a salad bar. Jane wears thin, elegant black clothes. Her fingernails shine; her scarlet lips purse when she smiles. Her rich husband is a bad, bad man who will gain your trust in a real estate deal and take you down with him. Jane never wants to leave her house. She will talk on the phone, but it's hard to get her to come out to lunch. Unless I go visit her, I rarely see her. She spends her days watching rented shoot-'em-up videos and laughing, laughing when the bad guys win. Or the good guys, either one. Just as she laughed when Miss Stancil said, "No quiz!"

Yet isn't there understanding in that laugh, of a kind I haven't got yet?

"Do you remember Dorothy and Herman?" I say.

"Dorothy and Herman who? Hey, leave me some of that goat cheese, Laurie."

THEY HAD their parents' eyes. They had known longer than we had about the integration: I read it in their faces.

"Get away from the raisins!" boys yelled from the monkey bars at recess that first day, while Dorothy and Herman held hands in silent counsel on the playground. I watched as a sixth-grader—Andrea was her name, a preacher's daughter—lured Dorothy and Herman to a seesaw. The arch in Andrea's neck should have warned them. Once they were seated on the seesaw, decorously rocking up and down, Andrea reached out and punched Dorothy in the back, fast as a blink.

Dorothy felt it. Of course she did, but she didn't show it. She kept riding the seesaw, slowly, her eyes on her brother's. Herman lowered the seesaw to the ground. Together, he and Dorothy retreated to the edge of the playground, to the spot where Mr. Underhill had spoken to me. Andrea, with her best friend Marge, chased them and chanted, "Blackbirds! Mr. Underhill says you're blackbirds!"

Their mother did cleaning sometimes for my mother. Mama had praised her for the way she could iron a shirt. Their father had helped my father tear down a tiny old house in our backyard, and Daddy had let him have some of the lumber.

Jane and I had stood out back, watching the house come down, and I think Herman was out there too, helping his father.

"Who used to live there?" Jane asked my father.

"Oh, servants," Daddy said cheerfully, stacking the weathered green-painted wood, "servants for people long ago, people who had money. Not like us. We're poor folks."

So the old house came down. It was a fire hazard, Daddy said. He called the Negro man "Joe." Joe called him Mr. Spires. But even now, wouldn't that be all right, when one man employs another?

Seesaw, Margery Daw. How does the rest of that rhyme go? Was Andrea's friend really named Marge, or am I getting it mixed up with the rhyme?

"Go away," Andrea said after she hit Dorothy, and again after Herman led his sister away from the seesaw. Marge echoed, "Go away!" But Herman and Dorothy had already gone as far as they could, without running away from school. They ignored the taunts from the swingsets and the jungle gym, where children cavorted and hung upside-down.

I was with Jane, of course. I said the dumbest thing: "I bet Dorothy and Herman would like to climb the monkey bars, but nobody'll let them."

"It's too hard, anyway," Jane said in the reasonable way that I loved, "and it's not that much fun."

"Think of something fun," I said, feeling sick as I watched the brother and sister, severely composed, keep up a semblance of conversation with each other, out of earshot of the rest of us.

"I can't," Jane said. She was watching them, too.

"It was fun when Daddy tore down the old house," I ventured.

"No, it wasn't." Jane turned on me, her eyes flashing. "That could have been a great big doll's house for us, if your father had let us have it."

"He was afraid it would fall down on top of us," I said.

"And how would that have felt?" Jane asked accusingly, as if a caved-in house would have been my fault.

TAMMY'S PAGEANT was the same week as the hat theft and the integration, and at the last minute she changed her mind about what to wear.

"I want to be a hula dancer," she told her mother, who had lost so much weight in anticipation of the pageant that she looked like the praying mantis on Miss Stancil's desk at school, a dried mantis that a boy had found in a field, its hard, plated face all anxious. "I want a grass skirt and flowers in my hair."

Tammy's mother said, "But you'll have to learn a whole new dance, a hula dance, in just three days."

"I will," said Tammy.

And she did. Jane and I were her audience, while their mother played "Aloha Oe" on the thumpety piano and Tammy swayed her hips, shook her silvery curls, and minced around barefoot.

"You're really good," I couldn't help but tell her.

"Thank you," Tammy said, but she was accustomed to compliments. She had won beauty prizes before, but they were small-time ones. Little Miss Virginia was major.

"And it can't hurt that we know Mr. Underhill," Tammy's mother said for the thousandth time, with a rippling chord on the piano keys.

"Mr. Underhill," I said, his image lurching into my mind, the green stocking cap a pennant in his hand.

"Don't tell," Jane hissed at me.

"Play it again, Mama!" cried Tammy. "And this time, make it sound more like Hawaii."

She pronounced it "Ha-*wah*-yah."

The pageant was held at the Miller and Rhoads Tearoom. The tearoom had a real runway, where on weekdays, at lunchtime, stylish models showed off the store's latest fashions. Jane, her mother, and I watched in disbelief as Tammy was knocked out in round one, not even making the semifinals, despite the presence of Mr. Underhill with his bald head bowed beneath the lights of the runway and the fact of his chiefness in the whole row of famed, prominent judges.

A redheaded juggler from Norfolk got the judges' unanimous vote. I could swear she had breasts, though she was only seven. She looked dumb: her tongue poked out from her teeth. Yet she won.

Afterwards, heading back to the car, Tammy tore loose from her mother's handhold. She shredded the grass skirt so that her green panties flashed to all the other parents and contestants, many of whom sobbed as they raced to the sanctuary of their cars. Tammy's face was a wrecked palette of mascara and rouge.

During the ride home, while a last gardenia blackened in Tammy's hair, a conviction lodged itself in her mother's mind: the belief that Mr. Underhill wanted to kidnap Tammy.

"You stay away from him, you hear?" her mother said.

"I never even see him," said Tammy, who would not start first grade until September.

"I'm afraid he might try to get you," her mother said. "I have good instincts for this sort of thing."

In the back seat of the car, Jane widened her eyes at me. I thought she was incredulous, as I was, at her mother's remark.

Instead, she was gazing raptly past me, at an old downtown bridge with stone arches.

She said, "It's beautiful, isn't it?"

"No more pageants, Tammy," their mother declared, "not when the judges are kidnappers and crazies."

"But Mama," Tammy bawled, "I want to be Cleopatra next time."

Jane let her head fall back and stared at the bridge as we drove beneath it. "Beautiful," she whispered.

JANE STARTED finding beauty everywhere: the toilets, for example, in the school restrooms, toilets which were cracked porcelain affairs from the nineteen-teens. Their design was so graceful, Jane said. There was beauty in the amber light of afternoon when we rode our bikes, and she used the word *amber* proudly. Miss Stancil's voice was beautiful, Jane said, when she led the class in the Pledge of Allegiance. "Notice it, Laurie," she said, "such a pretty, clear voice, with the same local accent that you and I have got."

How did Jane at ten know about local accents, our accents, apart from the way other people talked?

And Herman's face. Herman was beautiful, Jane said: "See the way his cheeks are round, but the rest of his face is thin."

"I'm going to tell him you said so," I said.

"I already did," she said. "I love Herman. I told him that, too."

We watched as he tossed a ball to Dorothy, a blue ball they had evidently brought from home, their wrists poking out of their coat sleeves. Dorothy was as tall as a grown woman.

I said, "Does Herman love you back?"

"I'm not telling you," she said. "I know better than that."

Beyond that day, I have no clear memories of Herman, and only one more of Dorothy. She was in my home ec class in high school. I can see her bent over her sewing machine, feeding bright cloth to the needle, her foot working the electric pedal.

In the restaurant, twenty years after saying she loved Herman, Jane smiles as she says, "Tell me the rest of the story, Laurie, but fast, because I have to get on home."

"I hated Mr. Underhill," I said, "because of Herman and Dorothy. I never spoke to either one of them. That was my fault."

"I just don't remember that," Jane says. "I do remember that pageant, when Tammy didn't win." And she chuckles.

MR. UNDERHILL did one other extraordinary thing.

This was at Christmastime of my junior year, when Jane and I were going to the big high school that served the whole county. By then, Mr. Underhill and Miss Stancil were far, far behind us. Mr. Underhill never kidnapped Tammy. He quit his job as principal and was teaching geography at a small private school. He lived at the old hotel, which hadn't been a hotel for about fifty years and was instead a rental property for the humble, just a few families in the big drafty building—though Mr. Underhill surely had enough money to live somewhere else had he wanted to. He'd gotten funny over the years, as my mother put it, getting so very quiet, he who had once burst into classrooms and held assemblies.

Back in the glory days of the hotel, so the legend ran, a deer park had surrounded it, and sure enough, the descendants of those deer were still around, shy creatures living in the nearby forest. Walking very quietly in the woods, you might glimpse one. Somehow, Mr. Underhill captured two of them and put them in a homemade wire pen outside the old hotel, a large comfortable pen equipped with hay and a water trough and strung with Christmas lights. A sign said, "Santa's Reindeer."

I loved the deer. I went every afternoon to visit them, to reach through the pen and pet their noses if they'd let me. They were magical, splendid, and amazingly tame—two small does. They smelled like the woods, and their eyes, when they met mine, were so gentle that I wanted to cry.

Everybody went to look at them, feeding them carrots and apples and sugar cubes and calling them reindeer, even though they didn't have antlers. Their pen was the center of Glen Allen in those days before Christmas.

Every morning when I rode the bus to school past the old hotel, I saw Mr. Underhill out front tending to them. Jane didn't ride the bus. She had a wild boyfriend, Dave Becker, who drove her to school and back. Some days they didn't make it to school.

Jane and I led busy lives. We had "school spirit." We sang in the glee club and had parts in the class play. We were cheerleaders, even though we thought our orange uniforms were ugly. We brushed our long hair flat and wore thin black ribbons around our necks. And all the boys were after Jane.

Even the young, handsome history teacher, Mr. Wells, seemed to have a crush on Jane. I was madly in love with Mr. Wells. I dreamed of going to the prom with him, of sneaking kisses, of having as many babies as he wanted.

He pointed out that our neck ribbons were not a new fashion. "During the French Revolution, aristocratic ladies tied red ribbons around their necks to mock the guillotine," he said, stopping Jane and me in the hallway one day, as people rushed around us.

I grinned at him, waiting for Jane to flirt back. She always knew what to say. But she snapped, "Don't talk to *me* about death."

She grabbed my arm and hustled me down the hall with her. "I just can't stand it, is all," she said, pulling the ribbon off her neck and throwing it to the floor.

"What's going on, Jane?" I said.

"It's stupid old Dave," she said. "He said how much fun it would be to shoot those reindeer. He's got a bow and arrow. I broke up with him this morning, but it's all I can think about—that he might do it."

"He better not," I said, my stomach lurching.

"Let's go check on the deer," Jane said, "right now."

"How? We don't have a car."

"We'll get Mr. Wells to drive us," Jane said, as if this were routine.

We found him in his empty classroom, eating lunch from a paper bag. He listened gravely to Jane's story, and then he did drive us, cutting out of school in mid-day to take us back to Glen Allen in his van. Snow was falling, but melting as it hit the windshield. Jane sat up front with him and I sat in the back, thinking, even through my fear for the deer, how fascinating Mr. Wells was, how much he knew. He pointed to a sweet gum tree and said that during the Civil War, with candles in short supply, Southerners soaked the round green seedpods in lard and used them instead, lighting the stems for wicks.

Jane said, "But still, they lost."

"You could have said *we* lost, Jane," said Mr. Wells, "but you didn't. Interesting."

"Oh, it was so long ago," Jane said, "and war is so boring."

"Not really, on either count," he said, pulling up in the yard of the old hotel.

"They're gone!" I cried.

We tumbled out of the van. The pen was empty, its chicken-wire walls and log corner-posts stripped of the Christmas lights and hay. The dirt floor was covered with hoof prints, as if the deer had danced there, or struggled to get away from Dave Becker and his bow and arrow, but there was no blood.

"Where are they?" said Jane.

"I let them go," said a voice behind us. We turned and found Mr. Underhill standing there, burly as ever, his arms crossed over his chest. "They were restless," he said. "It was never my intention to make them unhappy. I took them back to the woods."

Jane burst into tears and hugged him, while his arms dropped to his sides and his checkmark eyebrows rose up and up. How long had it been since anybody hugged him?

"I'm so glad," Jane said. "Thank you."

"I've got to get back to school. We all do," said Mr. Wells. "Laurie, Jane, let's go."

"I'm not going back," I said.

Jane released Mr. Underhill, wiped her eyes, and said, "Laurie, we've got cheerleading practice!"

"You go on," I said, turning away from her. "I'll call you tonight."

"Aren't you glad about the deer?" she said. "What's the matter, Laurie?"

"Of course I'm glad," I said, and I was. A sob of relief hovered in my chest, right by my heart. So what was I mad about? "Go on."

And she and Mr. Wells rolled away in his van.

"I REMEMBER now, I do!" Jane's eyes meet mine fully, her mouth an O of surprise. She counts out a big tip for the waitress. "I remember Mr. Wells driving us out there. So what happened next? Did you call me that night?"

"No," I say. "I had too much on my mind. I kept wondering if you and Mr. Wells had pulled over in that van and, you know, taken advantage of it. He was damn good-looking."

"Laurie!" she hoots, swinging her head over her empty plate of cream cake. "He was never my type. Look, I've got to go."

She hugs me and takes off, shrugging a black shawl around her shoulders, shaking back her blonde hair. On the table is the little Styrofoam box that the waitress brought for Jane's leftover sun-dried-tomato ravioli. "Jane, you forgot something," I call after her, but she's gone—fast—just like she and Mr. Wells had left, once they knew the deer were safe.

In retrospect, in make-believe, I confront Mr. Underhill. I say, "Stocking cap," and he grovels. I ask how he caught the deer, and he tells me a secret, that all he had to do was step into the woods and open his arms. I say, "Blackbirds," and his confession is ringing and passionate.

But I was sixteen, and melodrama was too tempting, too everlasting, to resist. The van was far down the road, Jane's waving hand still visible. I knew Mr. Wells was talking to her in his urgent way, and that they would not miss me one bit. My anger fell in on itself like the little torn-down house.

"I'm never going back to school," I told Mr. Underhill.

"Sure you will, Laurie," he said, as if we talked about this all the time, "and it'll be grand."

The sun came out as I turned and left him. I headed home, telling myself I was letting him off easy because it was Christmastime, that another day I would punish him as he deserved. Sunlight caught in the trees, and I was the only one on that old, narrow road, so how could I help but be happy?

Sailor's Valentine

Let us begin with two islands called Male Island
and Female Island.

—Marco Polo, *The Travels*

BOB WILLIAMS, DRUNK for seven years, surprised his
wife by sobering up and opening a candy store in an abandoned boxcar that had sat for years beside the railroad tracks.
He got the proper licenses, cleaned the place up, and made all
the candy himself, old-fashioned sweets such as fondant, pra-
lines, toffee, butter creams, and maple fudge.

He was handsome again, Brandy saw, for he had shed his
gut. His black hair grew in a shock past his ears. Nine years
they'd been married, and now Bob was thirty-six and Brandy
twenty-six, still her same small-boned, nut-blonde self, still
barren. Her parents had died of pneumonia the year before,
not in the winter but in the spring, within a week of each
other, leaving the blue house that Brandy and Bob had shared
with them not just to Brandy, but to Bob, too. That surprised
her; she hadn't thought they liked him.

The blue house sat right beside the railroad tracks, close enough to the boxcar that Brandy could see Bob's every move through its long open sliding doors. She watched him at night when he worked in the glow of yellow light, stirring vats of chocolate and rolling out almond paste on a marble-top table. For two years now, even before her parents died, she and Bob had slept in separate rooms—hers the one they used to share, the room she'd had as a child and all her life, and Bob in the downstairs den that Brandy's father had kept as an office and had yielded to his son-in-law. The den contained a sofa and a cot, but Bob slept on the floor. Once or twice, Brandy had tiptoed to the threshold and found him stretched out on his back, sound asleep, dressed in the clothes he had worn all day. He had slept so much from the drinking, all the early years of their marriage, that he looked young and fine and rested.

Now he kept long hours at the candy store, and he was so happy he sang, which she had never known him to do. He sang the old songs that he had learned as a child in the elementary school they'd both attended, only he'd gone there ten years earlier than Brandy. He sang "Supper on the Grass" and "Bring Me Little Water, Sylvie" and "John Jacob Jingleheimer Smith," which got on her nerves so bad she finally went out to the boxcar and asked him to stop.

It was early morning. In her nightgown and bathrobe, she climbed up the steps, stuck her head in, and saw him pressing pecans into a pan of fudge, licking a big wooden spoon.

"Breakfast," he said.

"You woke me up," she said.

"It's time you got up anyway," he said. "I wish you'd help me, Brandy. Make the candy and sell it with me."

She had held two jobs for a long, long time, while Bob was too drunk to complete the house painting he'd contracted for, and now the habit of work was as strong in her as her love for Bob had been when she was sixteen and wild for him. "How do I know this will last?" she asked him, in the dim morning cool of the boxcar while a mockingbird trilled outside. "This store might fold. You might start drinking again. Why did you stop, Bob? What turned you off from it?"

"I had enough," he said. He put the fudge away to cool. "Do you want me to start again?"

"I never knew you had so much willpower," she said, but she didn't mean it as a compliment. She felt instead that he was keeping secrets from her, that before her very eyes he had changed into somebody else, while she was still stuck in her barren body, living in the room she'd had as a child.

Bob said, "Some people count the days they've been sober. I don't. It just doesn't attract me anymore. I can even cook with it and not want any."

"Well, stop singing that damn song. You know the one I mean," Brandy said, and stumped away from him. She heard Bob's laughter behind her, back in the boxcar. She'd never even known he could make candy or that he wanted to sell anything or that he planned to start a business of his own. She'd thought she knew him: a big drunken wreck of the good-looking man she'd married. Now he wasn't the wreck or the bridegroom, either one. Who was this sleek stranger who charmed his customers?

As she reached her house, the seven a.m. train shot by, steaming and shrieking and churning. People often asked her, "How can you stand to live so close to the tracks?" but she loved it. She would not have lived anywhere else. She went inside and got ready for her job as a school secretary. Her other job, bookkeeping for two churches, she did at home.

Dressed in everything but her shoes, she went to a front window and regarded the old hotel on the other side of the tracks. It was still as proud as in the days when it was grand. She realized that Bob, who had been obsessed with the hotel for years, had not talked about it in a long while. At one time, he chronicled its history in scrapbooks, worshiping its creator, a Confederate captain who died disappointed that the hotel never drew enough guests. Brandy squinted, staring at it. Pigeons roosted on its balconies, and its broken windows sparkled. For a long time, the hotel had been her rival, and now Bob was neglecting it.

"I don't have time for that," she said and jammed her feet into her shoes. She was late—she who was never late.

All morning at work, typing papers for the school principal, she thought about Bob and his newness. Be glad for him, she told herself, it's what you've wanted for so long. She remembered being sixteen and in love with him, when all other men and boys seemed uninteresting to her, even a little foolish. Now she felt like the biggest fool of all.

The truth was, his happiness galled her and so did his success. For he was successful. Customers bought the candy all day long, from the first day he opened the shop. Yet *she* had supported *him* for so long, that she felt she'd be angry for a hundred years, whether he worked or not, whether he stayed sober or not. She was still the hardworking, hoarding ant and he the grasshopper.

Hovering beside the desk, the principal said, "I hear Glen Allen might organize a Chamber of Commerce, with your husband as president."

"That'll be the day," Brandy said, slamming a drawer shut.

The drawer pinched her finger painfully, and she cried out, then said, "He was a lot more fun when he was drinking."

It wasn't true, but it made the principal turn away big-eyed and leave her alone. Typing, Brandy thought only of sabotage: she would put a rat in Bob's kettle and call the health inspector.

At lunchtime she went home, as she always did. A shock awaited her. There were Bob's scrapbooks of the hotel tossed out on the trash heap for burning. She pulled them out and marched to the boxcar.

Even before she reached it, she heard him singing a ditty from the old school songbooks: "Come away with me, Lucille, in my merry Oldsmobile . . ." She thought, there will be a girl in there with him, some dark-haired beauty whom he has found to love, some candy-making stranger whom he has known all his life and rediscovered. " . . . Auto-mo-bubbling, you and I," he sang. They'll be making candied violets, Brandy thought, and planning their future together.

But when she went inside the boxcar, Bob was alone, pulling taffy. He grinned at her and kept on singing, the pitch of the song deepening. The taffy gleamed purple in the sunlight.

Brandy waved the scrapbooks, which were heavy in her hands. "What are you doing?" she said. One book fell to the floor and opened to a picture of Captain Cussons hammering stakes into a hayfield, stakes that bore the names of streets, laying out his plans for Glen Allen. Black-and-white grasses swayed frozenly in the whiteness that was the sun of 1868, long before the hotel was even begun; the stake said "Mountain Road." "How can you throw these out? I thought you loved that place," she said. "You've got the most complete record of its history that anybody's ever made."

"You save those scrapbooks if you want to," said Bob. "I'm going to make a candy model of the hotel, out of gingerbread and marzipan."

They stood in the sunlit boxcar with the smell of the candy all around them, and Brandy thought: this is a riddle, some question I didn't ask. Why do you sleep downstairs, Bob, why do you stay with me at all? He was an escape artist who had gotten out of chains and handcuffs underwater, while she was still caught there, struggling. The old hotel was where they used to make love, long ago before they were married; they'd made love so many times in its high, empty rooms.

She took the scrapbooks in her arms and carried them back to the house, where she put them on the upper shelf of the hallway closet. An obsession pitched away: what would become of it? Would she herself catch it, like a softball or a fever? She pushed the scrapbooks to the back of the shelf.

He was powerful, and not only because he was still young and strong, rejuvenated, and not only because he was her husband who slept downstairs and sang to himself while he made candy. Even if he grew old and sick, he would be powerful in his new way.

She stood in front of the closet and heard the flag snapping lazily on the flagpole all the way down at the post office, but other than that, how silent it was, her house and Glen Allen all around her. Her parents' voices still echoed in these rooms somewhere, her parents who were buried behind the Baptist church. Echoed to silence, those voices, but Brandy felt them. She felt her mother sigh: *No children, nor will there ever be.*

Barren: such an old-fashioned word. Yet she didn't want to adopt, to bring into her midst some stranger's brat, some bad seed, for she felt sure it would be bad, that she would be unlucky. She and her mother had talked about that, hadn't they? Memory failed her. Panic spread through her body in a dark flood.

Small-boned and nut-brown, she was. Never meant to bear a child. As a little girl herself, she'd picked out names for the babies she planned to have some day, beautiful names she loved—Ambrose and Mary Ellen.

Oh Brandy, put the windows down, came her mother's voice, but her mother was dead. *Don't you hear the wind rising? A storm's coming,* and like a mechanical doll, her nut-brown legs joint-popping at the ankles and knees, as if she were still growing, she obeyed.

SHE DID not confide in anyone. To the outside world, how happy they must seem: a man contented in his work, his wife having him nearby all day long. Maybe she was lucky. Bob didn't keep snakes or set the house on fire.

After school let out each day, dozens of children paraded into the shop, and how could she resist? At last she pinned her hair back and put on an apron that covered all of her clothes, though she didn't cook the candy. She helped Bob sell it, so that the picture they presented to the world was complete, of mom-and-pop shop, a young couple making their way in the world. Bob kept his profits in a box that Brandy's mother had owned, a heart-shaped box that was decorated with beautiful ridged seashells.

The children veered away from Brandy. Their eyes slewed away from hers when she counted the change into their hands and wrapped up the sweets. They wanted Bob.

"Tell me your dreams," he said to them, and Brandy at first said, "Don't. Don't do that, Bob," so sharp he looked up at her, for she said it in her mother's voice. She feared the children's parents might misunderstand, might think Bob meant to drag the children's secrets out and hurt them, might accuse him of putting sugary hands on their little ones.

Bob paid her no mind. He said, "Kids, don't tell me the dreams everybody has, the ones about falling or losing your teeth or being naked in a public place. Those old familiar dreams—why, they go all the way back to the days of ancient Greece." He paused, wiping sugar off the countertop, and the children gazed at him in awe, for their parents always shooed them away when they told their dreams, and never talked about ancient Greece. Bob said, "I want your strange ones, those and only those. Don't try to palm off any TV stuff on me."

A child with eyes too big for her face said, "I dreamed I turned into a fire engine," and Bob cried, "Yeah!" and gave the little girl a peppermint stick, striped like a barber's pole, which she stuck between her lips like a cigarette.

The children didn't want to talk to Brandy, but old ladies did, for they too had discovered the shop. They wore all black, just as they had done since Brandy's childhood, these sibilant creatures who smelled of dust and lemons and cut crystal. They talked their old talk to Brandy, so that at night their voices rang in her ears and she saw again their open mouths with the tongues dark like parrots'. To her they quoted their violent old cookbooks: "Kill a hen!" "Strain the clabber!" "Mash the bananas with a silver fork."

"Tell my husband, he's the cook," Brandy would say to them, wanting to steer them away from her, their black-clad bodies heavy or desiccated. They cleaved to Brandy, and Bob got the children and their dreams. The old ladies brought recipes for brown sugar sand dollars (confections so sweet Brandy thought her teeth would scream) and told of clocks that chimed only when family members died, and soon

Brandy had quit both her jobs to be at the candy store all the time, though her heart beat so fast she thought she would die, die as the train raced past with its wind and thunder, soot staining the white desert of her apron and the white clicking shine of Bob's teeth. The train going by: hearing it, that was the only time she prayed.

Her racing heart was new.

"Tell me your dreams," Bob said, and the children did.

The old ladies were too old to die. They went to all the funerals in Henrico County; they had come to those of Brandy's mother and father. Brandy's mother had admired them, had inherited them from her own mother, these elegant crows whose families (Broaddus, Sheppard, Scott, Christianson) had been in Glen Allen forever, their fortunes rising and falling, and whose husbands had died so long ago that they had scarcely existed. The old ladies had known Captain Cussons, they claimed; he had loved them when they were beautiful girls.

They fought among themselves about how Captain Cussons had died, Cussons the founder of Glen Allen: "It was yellow fever, when he was on a visit to Memphis." "No, he fell and broke his neck climbing the steps to the east tower, see, look where I'm pointing at his hotel, he broke his neck and his niece found them, the niece that went to Paris and was never heard from again."

Bob snapped his head up from dipping candied orange peel in chocolate and said, "The Captain died of pneumonia in January 1912."

"Pneumonia," said an old lady around the sourballs in her mouth. "A goose just walked over my grave. Pneumonia is what will get me, I know it now." To Brandy, she said, "Your poor mother and father."

Brandy watched and listened and her thoughts were at once right there and far away. She thought: the answer to the riddle will be whether or not he comes to me in the night, ever again. Of course, she herself could go to him, any night at all, could tiptoe down to the den where he lay sleeping on the floor, wedged between her father's old desk and the rosewood bookcase with carved feet like a vulture's, carved feet that had scared her as a child and scared her still. Would she find Bob lying there, or a lump of fondant dressed in Bob's clothes, a gingerbread man with cinnamon hearts for eyes?

All around her, the talk turned back to sweets. "He can candy anything," the old ladies said to Brandy fiercely. "He made candied onions yesterday. Delicious!" The old ladies were jubilant these days, raucous even, the sugar running through their veins like sap. Old ladies and children all day long: Brandy and Bob were never alone. The only thing she could think of to say to him was so awful that she was glad for all the people around, so she did not say it: "I'm the goose on your grave, Bob."

Screening out the old ladies' talk, she listened to the children chatting to Bob. A boy said, "I dreamed I set a green lion free from a zoo," and another one said, "I was on a roller-coaster that crashed," and another said, "You lie! If it crashed in your dream, you'd be dead." Bob rewarded them with lime and cherry gumdrops, and meringues with silver icing piped around the sides.

"It's a craze," an old lady said to Brandy about the buying of dreams, her breath sharp with age and licorice, "just like the children have their own crazes, thumb-wrestling and such. If he gives away too much of his candy, how will you make any money?"

"I wonder about that myself," Brandy said, but it seemed that the more candy Bob gave away, the more money he made.

"Let me see that box," the old lady said, seizing the shell-covered cash box. "Why, it's a sailor's valentine," she cried, running her thin hands over it. "Sailors made these on their long voyages, made them for their sweethearts. This is a very fine one, made so long ago."

She was the oldest of the ladies, so old that at birth, she liked to say, she'd been wrapped in a Confederate flag. She asked Brandy, "Can't you picture some sailor on the high seas, gluing these shells on the box to give to the girl he loved?"

"It was my mother's," Brandy said, "and her mother's before that."

"There's lint among the shells," the old lady said, and blew on the box so that dust flew up in bright motes.

SUMMER CAME and it was hot as a dream. Brandy decided it was time to do something with her parents' clothes, but she didn't know what. Her mother's things didn't fit her, and already her father's shoes had gone strange, the leather stiff and cracked; Bob's feet were too big for them. Soon the moths would find the clothes. The dresses and coats looked sad hanging deep in the closets, waiting to be taken out and worn into the world again. The house was dusty all over, and the clothes, even hidden away as they were, made Brandy sneeze.

She asked the old ladies, "What should I do?" and they said give everything to the church. So she did it. Bob helped her pack up everything in cardboard boxes that Brandy brought home from the grocery store, boxes that bore the names of Virginia food companies: Pocahontas tomatoes, Tidewater herring roe, Sauer's vanilla, Graves Brothers apples. Brandy stuffed her mother's pocketbooks with the editorials from the *Richmond Times-Dispatch* and wrapped them up in the funnies. Her heart was caving in. It was a hot Sunday afternoon with the smell of honeysuckle coming through the windows and the cicadas singing outside and a few wasps crawling on the pale ceiling of the room where Brandy's parents had slept. Brandy put on her mother's old plaid winter coat, closed her eyes, and hugged herself—to feel her mother's embrace again, in the familiar cloth. So hot it was, in the sunny room, in the plaid coat. Sweat and tears mixed on her cheeks. She bent her head toward the boxes as she packed the coat away.

Bob hummed while he helped Brandy. He looped her father's ties around his neck and said, "I'll keep some of these to remember him by." Everything else went to the church, where it was given out to people who were poor.

Sometimes, in the years that followed, Brandy would see her mother walking ahead of her on the road, but it was only some woman wearing her mother's plaid coat. Brandy would wave as she drove by, and the stranger would wave back—her mother's arm, her mother's coat, who could say?

AND STILL the train came through, five or six times a day and more at night, the train she could run away on. All those years of her growing up, it had shot cometlike past her house; all the years when she was in school, she had heard it and it was a summons she understood. She was its witness for all her years, had known forever that she could hop on it and leave. She imagined that it carried the same cargo it had hauled for a hundred and fifty years—same coal, same lumber, same passengers with their profiles bent toward their books—and the crewmen might be the same as in the days of Captain Cussons, ageless engineers flying up and down the rails. If for an instant the train would stop, she might see that the riders wore the styles of a hundred years ago—watch chains and black brocade for some, yeoman's boots and burlap for others—and that the sweet splintery timber came from some virgin forest deep in the Dismal Swamp, that the heaps of anthracite in the coal cars had changed, over time, into black diamonds. She used to make up stories about the train when she was little and couldn't sleep, or when she sat at her desk at school and heard its whistle and felt homesick, though her house was only a mile away and the school was friendly. She had wanted to be home in the blue house, smelling the tar and sulphur in the hurricane wind from the train. The train was truth; it would flatten her to a hot dime on the tracks.

So now, she told herself: I could just get on it and run away.

What to take with her? What would she want? A box of Bob's maple fudge, for she'd developed a taste for it; the carved claw feet of her father's bookcase; all the lilacs from her yard that bloomed early every spring; the family of shy wild cats that came out of the woods at night to eat the scraps she left for them; the screech owls and whippoorwills that she had heard forever; and the salty well water which visitors disliked, which her father had been so proud of, which had turned Brandy's teeth pale maize in childhood and kept them strong. Put all those things in any sack and it would be so heavy she'd fail in her leap to catch the train.

She thought about this as she sold candy in the boxcar, and she felt the old ladies reading her mind, condemning her. The only way to go would be to leave everything behind. Her own thin self she could manage. Her small nut-brown body could make it, jumping and clinging no matter how fast the train hurtled by, hanging on till she blacked out and woke up where? Far off in a city where she was no one, not herself, not her past, not Brandy at all, anymore.

BECAUSE OF her racing heart, she stopped eating candy. She had not gained weight; she never did. But her fast heart scared her, so she went to the doctor, who listened to her chest and gave her pills.

"You'll be fine," he told her. "You don't have to do anything different."

"I'll never have a baby, will I?" she said. "I've been hoping for the longest time."

"We did tests, didn't we?" the doctor said. "A few years ago. We could run some more."

"No," Brandy said.

"You can be happy without a baby," the doctor said.

She wasn't thinking about babies the way she used to do. Instead she thought about running away. Driving home with the bottle of pills in her lap, she thought that even in the act of escape, in the headlong triumph of rail riding, maybe what she would really want would be to come on back. She drove to her house, parked in the yard, and swallowed one of the pills in her dry throat. It tasted like a sandy kiss and made her cough.

Yet her heart kept racing, though she took the pills twice daily as the doctor had told her to do. Her heart was a wild live thing, taking over, beating its marathon life out of time with the rest of her, so that she pressed her hand over it and breathed slow and deep till the wild spells passed, as they always did eventually, leaving her weak and flushed and sweaty, laughing at the children who poured out their dreams for Bob: "I dreamed me and my brother weren't nothing but two heads talking in the sand," a big boy said.

FALL CAME and with it the mackerel sky that Brandy loved, the tight-packed zigzagged clouds of early morning, like a fish's scales. Bob made so much money that he took to keeping it in a sack. At day's end he'd empty it on the counter and run his fingers through it, the coins ringing as they hit the counter, the bills floating greenly for a moment aloft.

"Don't think this is why I run the store," he told Brandy one evening, when he saw her watching him.

"You do it for dreams," she said over her surging heart. She reached in her pocket, found a pill, and swallowed it with a swig of ginger ale. "Bob," she said, and he looked up from the money. She found her voice then and said, "If I die, there'd be nothing on this earth to show I was ever here."

He came close to her as she stacked trays of nougat in the refrigerator, but he did not touch her. He stood with his arms folded across his chest and his gaze was on her now, his mouth straight and still. "What would you like to leave behind?" he said.

"I just feel empty," she said. "We go on and on together, but we don't have any children. Say it, Bob, we're not good together anymore."

"It should be better now," he said, "now that I've quit drinking. I don't think we'll ever have children, Brandy. We'll have to live with that."

"But we don't sleep together. Do you even want to?" she said. "Is there any point in it, anymore, now that we've given up?"

"I do want to," he said, to her surprise, and in silence they closed up the candy shop and stepped outside into the darkness. Bob reached up and closed the long sliding door of the boxcar with a clash that echoed back into the woods.

In bed that night, he asked, would it hurt her heart?

"No," she said, and smiled. When he turned to her, she had a memory: as a child, she had found a bottle of Benedictine in her father's gun closet and made a secret snack of it, alternating gulps of the liquor with bites of a chocolate bar. Faster and faster she ate and drank, with the fire and the sweetness in her mouth.

Dawn came, and Brandy heard her mother's voice as plainly as if her mother had stepped into the room: *Look, the sun is coming up, just as red.* When Bob awoke, Brandy said, "I don't think I slept at all."

"But you did," he said.

"I was not complaining."

She buried her face in his neck and cried, all the sorrow flowing out of her. Outside, the crows were cawing, and inside, her mother was saying, *This is a fine warm house. It has stood so many winters.*

The Interview

LELAND RICHARDS WAS twenty-three, a farm boy from the Virginia Tidewater. Curiosity drew him to Niagara Falls in the summer of 1860, and the roar made him jump right in. The water yanked every limb from its socket. Just in time, rescuers hauled him out with ropes and pulleys. Summoned to the banks of the Falls, a doctor knelt beside Leland, rolled him over to expel the water from his lungs, and popped his arms and legs back into place.

Newspapermen couldn't get enough. "Miracle Man," ran one headline.

"Did Niagara Falls call your name?" asked one reporter, a woman with a twist to her lips.

"You could say it called me," he said. Her eyes distracted him, and her lovely ears, showing beneath her hair. Joy began at his toes and spread up through his body. "Miss," he said, "I'm a happy man. I went from being not unhappy, but you could say I failed to appreciate, go ahead and write this down, I failed to appreciate my life."

"I suppose you'll become a minister," the woman said, tapping her teeth with her pencil. Leland knew that his mother, ever aware of the importance of a woman's teeth and skin, would have put a stop to the tapping.

"A minister. No," he said.

The whirlwind had stripped him naked. Boys had fished his trousers out of the water—with his name still sewed to the waistband, thanks to Nancy, the woman back home who with her husband and family helped on the farm. Other reporters had asked if he had slaves. Nancy and her family were slaves. It was how it was. Thoughts of home fueled his buzzy gladness.

The woman reporter said, "I can't leave until you tell me something new, something you haven't told anybody else."

Sunlight rolled through the windows of the hotel parlor in eye-watering brilliance. The landlady hovered, offering cold spiced cider. The landlady was no longer charging him. The Miracle Man was a luminary, good for business. A haberdasher had provided a new suit. A dentist pulled for free a tooth that was bothering him. Confectioners sent candy and nuts.

The reporter accepted a glass of cider and sipped it. She had a hitch in her voice and in her walk, though Leland wouldn't say she limped. For a short girl, she had a long stride. "It's not fair," she said. "People will pay attention to anything you say."

The parlor was filling up with honeymooners ready for card games and piano playing. Leland stood and guided the reporter out onto the porch, where rocking chairs seesawed to the motion of guests' vigorous behinds and legs.

"This is not the story I want to write," the woman said, frowning. "I want to write about war. I can smell it coming."

He took that for a farewell, but she had more to say.

"Have you thanked the men who saved you?" she asked.

"Of course." He wanted the men to fish with him some-day on the York River. He pictured them in his boat, with this woman back on shore where voices would reach her. In his mind, it was a mild gray day, with dogwood white on the bluffs above the river.

She barely came up to his shoulder. With his hands, he measured the difference in their height. She would not be jollied. She finished her cider and set the glass on the porch railing.

"How old are you?" he asked.

"Nineteen."

"I have a sister your age," he said.

Two rocking chairs became vacant, and they sat down. He said, "When we were little, my sister and I, we used to play store. One would be the merchant, the other the customer."

"That doesn't give me the story I'm after," she said, but she was rocking right lively.

"All right," he said. "That sound. It was like voices. Laugh-ing. An explosion that went on and on. It was what I'd been waiting for."

She was writing.

"Longer I listened, the louder it got. You know how a shell sounds when you hold it to your ear?" Her lovely ear. She nodded. He said, "I answered that call."

She put her pencil down and rested her chin in her hands.

She was a question mark, what with all the questions she asked, and a question mark was the shape her body made when they danced together that evening in the hotel parlor, and she was a question mark in marriage, when she lay with him. Her parents' wedding gift was paper and pens and ink, so she could write to them.

Her name was Octavia. *My dear wife,* he wrote from camp. He wore a pair of wire mesh spectacles that he found in a field. The mesh tempered sunlight and dust.

Since recovering from measles, he had been assigned the duties of a quartermaster's clerk. The work suited him. His commander looked into Leland's heart and divined thrift. Blankets, shoes, buttons, coffee. Not enough of anything. Soap, thread, tobacco. Horse liniment in attractive brown bottles. The hoarding and doling out, it got to him some days. He set aside a shelf in his office for lone, prized items: flyswatter, box of mourning stationery, rug beater. He counted bullets, tallying them in hundreds with a mark on his hand.

Only a magician could supply enough, he wrote Octavia.

Witch hazel for piles. Camphor. Boot polish. Bayonets and glue.

If General Lee came in right this minute and asked for lamp oil, a toothbrush, and sheet music, I could put his order together in a minute, long as he's not picky about the music.

He had more letters from his sister, Emily, than from his wife.

What you do now, for the army. Is it like when we played store? Emily wrote. *Remember we used acorns for money, and for wares, we had things Mother gave us. Commonplace things— chipped plates, dull scissors, watch fobs Father no longer wanted.*

Nails and paint, turpentine and salt. A tin of chocolate powder. He pried it open, dipped a finger in it, and licked the glorious bitterness. He dreamed of a honeycomb and woke slapping at bees, but it was February and he was in the mountains, the Blue Ridge sharp and purple.

"How much rope, Leland? How much hay?" the commander asked him when they passed, and it was better than a game, because Leland always knew.

Candles, dye, canvas, lye. Burlap and barrels, shovels and staves. Never enough. He burned a shipment of spoiled lard. The men would have eaten it.

Would that I had bins of extra limbs and boxes of eyeballs, he wrote Octavia, thinking she deserved to know. *Yr aff. Husband.*

He pictured his sister and his wife at home on the farm, with his mother. His father was long dead. He imagined his wife and his sister playing store, as he and Emily had done in childhood, and it was for them that he did his job well, for the store-players, the shrewd tiny merchants. *It is lasting forever and ever,* he wrote in the fall of 1862, when it had been months since his last furlough. The windfalls he received from generous families were foolish: dozens of mousetraps, a box of cardboard-soled slippers in too-small sizes. He bought fried pies from a sutler and got sick from them. One of the men claimed that the pies were made from dog meat, and Leland believed him. With his own eyes, he saw the date on a shipment of hardtack: 1812.

Time for the mesh sunglasses and a letter home.

My dear wife, he wrote Octavia. *Ask Emily if she still has the dibble. Mother let us use it for Store. Emily did not know what it was and I told her, for planting. It cost her many acorns.*

Would you quit writing about that damn game and tell me about the war, Octavia wrote.

He was fighting again, for he was fully well. He was promoted to major. One day he had one of the rare letters from his mother: *It is how I have felt all my life a war going on the men away the hands run off it is almost a relief Son now that it has happened for it matches up with how I have felt inside all ways, Yr. Loving Mother, Frances Abigail Whitten Richards.*

One day he had word from his sister that their mother had fallen ill and died. *Octavia and I and the preacher dug the grave. It took a long time. The preacher is old and I was afraid it would be too much for him. We had only two spades so one rested while the others worked.* Emily enclosed a package of horehound candy. He unwrapped a piece and sucked on it as he read. Her letter concluded, *Octavia has grown taller. You will be surprised.*

When the war was over and he got himself home, the woman who greeted him at the door of his farmhouse was nearly a foot taller than he was: Octavia.

When the war was over. After the war. As if saying, "After breakfast." Nobody should have to say that.

AFTER WE were married, my wife grew. After I got home again, once the war was over, I saw this myself. She was—is—still beautiful. Just tall. The tallest person I have ever seen.

Even as he stood at his own doorstep, holding his breath and looking up into Octavia's eyes, these sentences ran through his head as if he were writing a letter. He was too accustomed to letters to let go of the habit. All during the war, nothing had been more real than a letter. Maybe if he'd been wearing the mesh sunglasses to meet Octavia at the door, he would have been less shocked. Encountered through tiny screens of wire, the tall stranger might have loomed less.

Was this what the roaring Niagara tried to tell him, those five years ago? For it was a personal cry, that volume of sound that beckoned him over the side. Meeting his wife at war's end, he remembered his exultation as he pitched himself into the water. During the war, the sound had become a tale he told himself, a marvel and a treasure he could take out and turn over in his mind. He could close his eyes and smell the cologne and flowers in the parlor of the Niagara inn. The roar came back to him in this homecoming, a day of unseasonable cool in early May, with the sky blue as a jay over his smaller-than-he-remembered-it farmhouse.

He spoke his wife's name and reached for her hand. Surely she was standing on a chair or on a footstool hidden beneath her long dress.

Of course I reacted when I saw her, but no I don't remember what I said. I did not, as the expression goes, believe my eyes.

A clattering wagon pulled up, and a group of people climbed down from it, shaking out their shabby clothes, then heading toward him and Octavia with the self-righteousness of those bent on diversion.

"They have to pay first," Octavia said—her first postwar words to him. "Take care of that, Leland. This is how we eat. It's how we live, Emily and I."

When he didn't answer, Octavia shooed him toward his task. "Go get Emily," she said.

Would Emily too have become a giantess? Was their farm some magnifying place, or was he cockeyed from war and journeying?

"Emily's hanging out wash, around back," Octavia said. "And Leland? Ask her to bring some water. We usually give people some, with syrup in it when we have it." To the visitors, she said, "Pay my husband. Then you may come in." She closed the door so that they might encounter her for best effect when she swept it open, seven feet tall in a patchwork dress. The visitors paid Leland amiably with a cardboard box of baby chicks and strolled into his house. From outside, he heard them gabble and gasp.

Most of the fighting I did was in Virginia, he wrote his imaginary correspondent, a recipient born in this instant, *so you may wonder how it was that I did not get home except for the occasional visit. You ask how it was I did not know of this great change. Well, I did have the one letter from my sister Emily, that mild warning, Your wife has grown taller. During the war, soldiers might gain height into their early twenties. I believed girls had their height by fifteen or sixteen. I assumed my wife was completing her growth and that this meant she was getting enough to eat. Though I was fighting in Virginia it was often far to the West, in the mountains, and when I was East, in Petersburg, the fighting was such that I could not leave. If I'd known, I'd have come home right away. To do something. I do not know what.*

The chicks made gleeful sounds. They were falling out of their box with laughter. He sank down on the grass of his own yard, amid the hilarious chicks. After a while, he got up and went around back to find his sister.

"Exactly how many times, during the war, did you see your wife?" This was a doctor in Norfolk to whom he took Octavia. The doctor measured and examined her, made her walk away from him and toward him, and then spoke privately to Leland. To Leland, the conversation felt like the letters he was always writing in his head.

"She said her parents are of normal size. Is that accurate?" the doctor said.

Leland nodded. Stern Yankees, a beribboned old lady permanently outraged over some slight, the father a sleek cat of a man, ears flattening and flickering with the town's news.

"Well," the doctor said. "This is rare enough."

"What causes it?"

"Perhaps some kind of imbalance in the body, or a catastrophe."

"Like the war?"

"I meant something more like a bad fall, a blow to the head. Even that's just a theory."

"She's had no such accidents that I know of," he said, thinking, I'm the one that almost drowned.

Can't I go to war again and come home again and find her as she should be? That box of baby chicks, why they pecked at each other and died, the whole batch. What was wrong, that they pecked each other to death, a batch of baby chicks?

"Is she through growing?" Leland asked the doctor.

"It's hard to say."

The doctor's office was located near a school. Children were outside in the schoolyard, at play. Rising and falling, their muted shrieks reached Leland through the windows. "Love me, love me," the voices seemed to cry.

Go back to the day I bought the ticket for the train ride north. The station floor was covered with peanut shells and the air smelled smoky, from a fire not far off. A farmer was clearing a field. Go to boyhood, to a rainy day when I sat in the hallway paging through a book with engraved illustrations and fell in love with the Falls. The book belonged to Papa.

"Be careful with her," the doctor said.

Octavia's head in its bonnet nodded far above him as they walked out of the doctor's office, down the street and away from the capering children.

I must be dreaming. No woman would greet her husband like that, say to a man home from war, "They have to pay first and then they can have a look at me."

"Love me," the children's voices chorused, distant now as Leland and Octavia paced farther from the school. "Love. Me. Love. Meeeeee."

They reached the train station, where an old man surveyed Octavia up and down, then said to Leland, "Must need stilts to climb up on her." Leland drew back his arm to sock him, but Octavia caught his elbow. Laughing, the man asked her, "How far your feet hang off the bed, honey?" A pod of snot hung in his nose, and he leered right up into her face.

"There was a knock on the window before your mother died," Octavia said one evening.

Emily nodded. "Three raps. We both heard it. We looked out the window, but there was nobody. No breeze, either."

"That was the morning of the day she died," Octavia said. "She passed away that night."

"I'd heard all my life about that knocking, but I didn't believe it," said Emily.

This was his life, and he was getting used to it. His mother was dead and his wife was grown tall. Emily was the same, as far as he could tell, though Octavia told him Emily took to cursing during the war, cursed so hard Octavia was afraid of her. He could not imagine such words coming out of his sister's mouth.

He had not allowed anybody to pay and to view his wife since that first day he was home. He was providing for his family, though they lived on sweet potatoes and fish. Octavia liked her yams almost burnt, loved the sugary blackened sap that rose from the flesh and crusted when cooked a long time. "Candy," she said, closing her eyes. "It's how the earth itself would taste if you put enough sugar in it."

He was two people now, the Falls survivor and the veteran, and his wife was two people, the young reporter and her alpine self. It was hard to keep up with them all. Working the fields brought a reward: the sound of the train whistle from miles off, the first bars of a beautiful song. And in bed at night, he still found sweetness with Octavia. But her breath burned his bare skin. Floorboards creaked differently than he remembered. He dreamed of wheat fields and cornfields like a rolling ocean, splendid and windy and gold. Sunday still came, and he and his wife and sister walked to church. There was no piano or organ, just people's voices as they sang the hymns. The church bell was gone, melted down for bullets.

The day he'd gotten home from war and found his sister hanging wash in the yard, crying because the sheets were muddy, he hugged her and spoke her name. She exclaimed over him, said she'd feared she would never see him again. Then she said something he didn't expect.

"Why do cats have that little nubbin of skin halfway up the back of their legs? Leland, why? It's like a little leather island," and she'd grabbed a kitten, tears on her cheeks.

What could you say to that? The kitten sprang from Emily's arms, leaving red scratches.

And now this new voice spoke in his head, as if somebody were after him, arguing, jabbing him in the brain.

How did the river taste?

Clean, almost salty, though it is not the sea. It's far from the ocean. I would have to think about that, about how it tasted.

That happiness. Did it last, the joy and certainty you felt in surviving?

I can't work things out with all this in my head.

All right. What foods did you dream about during the war?

Oh. That's easy. Pickles, cheese, brandy, sausages, applesauce, pears and peaches. Stop. I can't think to sing the hymn.

You should have heard them cursing, those women, when you were off at war. Not just Emily. Your wife too. Both of them were cursing when your mother died. She died with those words in her ears.

That's a lie.

You weren't here. Right funny when you think about it—them cussing, her dying.

He didn't know whose voice it was invading his thoughts or what to make of the struggle inside him, the quarrels taking place in his head. He didn't tell Octavia or Emily.

"It's part of their paws," he said to Emily at supper, and she raised her face to his, startled. "That little thing on a cat's leg," he said. "You asked me about it."

"Don't do me that way," she said, "pick up talk from so long ago that I've forgotten all about it. Now tell me something, Leland. What was it like to kill people? Those other soldiers?"

He chewed his food for a long time. "I used to pretend they were just little towers."

"And the towers fell?"

"They fell."

Emily hung her head.

He was waiting, and for what? For the train to play the song that its whistle suggested, to finish the tune begun by those sparse bars of music that carried miles to reach his ears. Waiting for his wife to top out, like a tree or a shrub that would get its height first and then fill out, like the snowball bush he and Emily played store beneath, as children.

Think back. Go way back. What did Emily used to call that snowball bush? Back in childhood, in the days of dibble and store?

Oh. She did have a funny name for it. Wait and I'll ask her—
No. You have to remember.

Mow-mow bush, that was it. Rhymes with cow. We used to cut the blooms off and make believe they were snowballs and throw them at each other.

That's good, Leland. Very good.

Do you know how bad it got? There was pipe-clay ground up in the hardtack. And alum. We could taste it, yet we still ate it.

Kill the commissary, hang the sutlers. Pity you in your little mesh spectacles, you couldn't stop thinking about your belly.

"Octavia," he said. "Let's go out in the yard."

They pushed their chairs away from the supper table, and she followed him. The air smelled of wood smoke. He led Octavia to the well. He had her pour bucket after bucket of water over his head, and he wouldn't tell her why.

HE WANTED to invite his Niagara rescuers to visit him. His old plan: to take them fishing.

"For God's sake," Octavia said. "How would we feed them?"

"We don't have to have them here," he said.

"Well, I do get lonely," she said. "Don't you think I'd like to go see Mother and Papa? They don't know how tall I've gotten."

"Would you come back?" he said.

"I'd come back," said Octavia.

But she made no plans to go. One day she said, "All those people who used to come and pay to see me? It was Emily they ended up watching. She is very strange. Haven't you noticed the way she twists her hands? Your mother knew about her."

"There's nothing wrong with her."

Octavia said, "Yes, there is. People watched her, and they knew."

He didn't summon the Niagara men, but they came anyway, brothers named Messier. They were traveling the South to visit Antietam, Fredericksburg, Petersburg, Appomattox. "It wasn't hard to find you," the older brother said. His beard reminded Leland of the frothy Falls.

"The selling's started," the younger Messier said. "Roadside stands selling belt buckles and such. The battlefields are stores now."

"How are my parents?" Octavia asked, serving cornbread and buttermilk. Outside, the men's horses and wagon filled up the yard.

"He's still writing his newspaper," the bearded brother answered. After a pause, he asked Octavia, "Did it hurt? To get so tall?"

"Don't answer that, ma'am," said the younger brother. "You should be famous for being beautiful."

Emily, sitting in a corner of the room with a cat on her lap, spoke up. "Was he heavy?" she asked the visitors, indicating Leland with a nod of her head. "When you pulled him out of the water?"

"Yes," the brothers said together. The older brother raised his arms in a gesture that made the muscles bulge through his shirt.

Leland was sorry to have caused such trouble. He said so.

Emily said, "He wants to marry me off. Either one of you will do."

The guests looked at each other and laughed. Emily joined in and so did Octavia, giggling at first, then howling, Octavia spilling her pitcher, Emily's cat springing from her lap, the

Messier brothers' mouths stretching, shoulders jolting. They all looked ill, beset, bewitched.

Leland went to Octavia and took the pitcher from her hands. He eased her down in her chair and said, "Shh now," but her face kept working. To the men, he said, "Let's go fishing."

Leland. Forget the river and the channel and the men in the boat and the women back on shore looking pretty. Let them laugh, and don't ask why.

This is hard, Leland said to the voice in his head.

Poor Leland. Listen to your wife. Pick out her voice from the others. She sounds the way she does when she gets all worked up, doesn't she? All worked up in bed?

He rushed the brother who was nearer to him, the bearded one, seized him and wrapped his hands around the man's throat. How was it the man kept on laughing? His breath smelled of buttermilk. His beard felt soft. Leland squeezed the laughter right out of him while he fought back, landing a kick in Leland's gut and straining to tear Leland's hands from his throat. The women were shouting. The younger Messier leaped on Leland's back, pounding him with his fists, until finally Leland let go of the other man, who coughed and clutched at his neck.

In the silence, Octavia reached out and righted the pitcher, which had spilled buttermilk over the table and onto the floor. Emily's cat crept forward and lapped the milk. They all listened to the lapping, the tiny neat sounds, until the cat stopped and sneezed.

"You're crazy," the younger brother said to Leland. The man's eyes took up his whole face, bulging eyes Leland would remember, a fine blue.

"We'll go, we'll go right now," the older brother said. His neck was red, his voice a rasp.

EMILY MARRIED the preacher who had helped to dig her mother's grave, and they moved away. Leland expected Octavia to grow until her head brushed the ceiling, like a star on a Christmas tree too tall for the parlor. But she stopped, and she carried herself with a grace that he preferred to her younger, pugnacious stride.

It was summer when she died, summer 1872, every afternoon a shower and then long lighted evenings. Hay, corn, and tobacco grew in such abundance that Leland hired a dozen people to work alongside him in the fields. At day's end, the hum of their activity ceased. Cicadas sang in the trees. Leland toed the earth, smelling rain.

Leland. You're all alone. The Falls forgot you long ago. Are you happy, Leland?

Yes, he answered, *I'm happy,* and the voice stopped, as if it had everything it wanted.

The Lost Pony

WEST TO THE mountains, east to the sea; I used to hear my lost pony running on the road at night, the pony I'd won at a raffle the day the Glen Allen Youth Center opened, the pony that brought me such brief glorious popularity and then jumped his fence and vanished. Run away or got stolen, who could tell? He haunted the road, invisible, gone wild.

One time I woke up at dawn, got dressed, and went outside. Dew gleamed on the grass, so beautiful. Down the long driveway I sped toward the creek, sure I'd find the pony drinking the cold water. He wasn't there. The milkman drove up the empty road and turned into my driveway. This was back when milk still came in bottles, capped with white paper. Waving and wide awake, the milkman passed me. He would drive up to my house and leave the milk on the porch, and I would drink it for breakfast.

Again I heard the pony's hooves clip-clipping, and I took off after the sound, swerving left on Mountain Road (so narrow, back then, a child could nearly span it with one foot in each ditch), ran panting as far as the railroad tracks and waited as a train rushed by; leaped across the hot rails then and cocked my head to pick up the hoof sounds. They led me past the old hotel, the landmark I loved most of all, to the school, quaint, red brick, built in 1909.

My third-grade teacher, Miss Genevieve, was already there, out in the yard. "Why, Lyndoll," she said, "it's only six-thirty."

"I heard my horse," I told her. "I was following him."

She had on my favorite dress, a gray one with yellow pockets. I had admired her ever since she'd clapped a stovepipe hat on her head to recite the Gettysburg Address. That morning, as if I'd done nothing unusual, she drove me home in her old black Plymouth, its fenders rounded like a camel's humps.

"You might still find that pony," Miss Genevieve said. "At any rate, you'll get beyond it," meaning my loss.

"Tell me about your lit-up hand," I said, and she obliged with my favorite story. Her brother had worked in New Mexico, at a secret place where bombs were tested, called the Sandia Mountain Laboratory. Miss Genevieve had visited him and observed an explosion.

"The flash was so terrible and bright, you could see every bone in your hand," she said. She held her arm up in front of her face, demonstrating, in the safe Virginia morning. "I had on special glasses, yet still I could see my bones."

She stayed for breakfast at my house. I told my parents and my sisters, "Miss Genevieve had herself X-rayed by a bomb."

A hand lit by fire was what I wanted then, as much as I wanted my pony back. Now, what I wouldn't give for breakfast with Mama again, she who whispered, "I've been waiting for you" when I rushed stumbling into her hospital room that last time, last summer: Mama took those chemo treatments and didn't even flinch. The morning I got up to chase the mysterious horse, Mama had cooked things to tempt my appetite: French toast, Tidewater brand herring roe from a can, and biscuits covered with golden-brown meringue, a recipe she'd invented to get her picky daughters to eat eggs, and which Miss Genevieve raved about. Mama didn't know where my pony was, either. None of us ever found out. For a while, I wondered if the pony was dead, if my parents knew he was dead and kept this a secret from me, but we weren't that kind of family.

I had to explain about my dawn walk, of course. For once I had an appetite for breakfast. Daddy listened with interest about the lit-up hand and then said, "Miss Genevieve, how come you get to school so doggone early?"

"It's my habit," Miss Genevieve said.

Mama said to me, "I'm glad I didn't know you were out running around. I thought you were still asleep in your bed."

Years later, I dreamed of the pony. My mouth was full of pebbles and the pony spoke to me, telling me why: "Because you're mortal."

LET ME tell you two episodes that I've never told anybody about. First, about the raffle where I won that pony. Sandy soil and pines and silence: such was the land before the Youth Center was created, with money given to the community by a rich old lady, Mrs. Beasley. By Mrs. Beasley's decree, a pavilion for picnics and dances was built, a pit was dug for a swimming pool, and the tallest swing set I'd ever seen was rooted into the ground.

On the Grand Opening Day, May 1, 1967, Mrs. Beasley proclaimed, "Now the children of Glen Allen, our lovely town, will have a place to play." Everybody clapped, from babies on up to the old ladies who always dressed in black, friends of Mrs. Beasley's.

Mrs. Beasley's two sons were there, sweating with the rest of the crowd in the spring sunshine. The older one, William, had been a child prodigy, composing piano music and giving concerts and making lots of money, then losing every bit of his talent by the time he turned thirteen. Now he was middle-aged, with one eye sad and one eye mad. Everybody knew he lived at home with his mother and didn't do a thing, and that the Youth Center really existed for the purpose of giving William a job, since he was to be its manager. He held a spotted pony by the bridle, clearly afraid of it. The pony would be the prize. I clutched my raffle ticket.

Mrs. Beasley's younger son, Gibson—"Gibby"—was a dwarf, and famous: he hadn't been home in years. An actor, he lived out in Hollywood. In his last film, he'd played a lawyer who had only to hold a briefcase, pass in front of an open door, and say a few words in a courtroom, to steal the whole show. He stood next to me, his rough head just below my own, and mocked his mother as she gave her speech. He made antic movements with his hands and mumbled, "For the *chil . . . dren* of Glen Allen" in a tremolo.

"Race you to the swings," Gibby Beasley said to me, and I did. We caught the long metal chains in our hands.

"Who is that pretty lady? And that one?" Gibby Beasley asked me as we launched into the air. He pointed at young women in the crowd. "I didn't go to school here," he said. "I went to boarding school in New England, so I don't remember anybody. Who is that beauty?" He pointed at Mama with one tiny, outstretched, booted foot.

"That's my mother," I snapped. "Leave her alone." I *could* snap at him; he was such a silly man, barrel-chested and bantering.

Pumping our legs, we sailed above the crowd. I saw Miss Genevieve present Mrs. Beasley with a bouquet of pink lilies. Over the applause, I heard crows cawing off in the pine woods. Gibby's swing criss-crossed past mine. Determined to outpace him, I swung ever higher.

Then it happened: I went right over the top of the swing set. I *wrapped*. Flying, I saw not only the Youth Center and all my neighbors and family and classmates oblivious below me, and Gibby's face, upturned in astonishment. I saw as well the whole town of Glen Allen, just a village really—all of its big old tumbledy houses, its cheap little tract shacks, its colored-people neighborhood with smoke unfurling from chimneys, the railroad tracks with a train puffing toward us from Ashland.

And I saw this vista not just as it was, in those few airborne seconds of 1967, but in some other time too. There was the old hotel with a lawn party in progress, all the guests wearing ruffly dresses and ice-cream suits, and among them strolled John Cussons, the Confederate Captain and hotel owner whom old Mrs. Beasley claimed to have known and loved. I recognized the Captain from photographs I'd seen. Raising his Panama hat from his long gray curls, he saluted me. There was the spotted pony hitched to a cart, hauling youngsters through the Captain's rose garden. I could smell the roses' slumbrous red scent, hear the guests' laughter, taste on my tongue the sherried cake they were eating, feel on my skin the pony's flying mane and the breeze from decades earlier.

Then the Ashland train shot down the rails and blocked my view, its whistle hooting, and I vaulted over the swing set and plummeted to earth with a jerk of the chains.

Gibby Beasley said, "Did you really do what I think you did? Nah." He scuffed his little boots in the grass below his swing. "Look, Mother's picking the winner of the pony. It'll be me. I bought fifteen tickets."

My parents had bought one ticket apiece for my two sisters and me. When old Mrs. Beasley trumpeted, "Lyndoll Harris," I leaped from my swing and darted toward the spotted pony, hugging his neck. How alive he was, with his warm nose and great gleeful eyes. "You even get a saddle," Mrs. Beasley said.

I led the pony to Mama. She bent down to smile at him but she wouldn't touch him. When my sisters clamored for a ride, I dreamily surrendered the pony.

In the weeks thereafter, I rode the pony before school, after school, and after supper. Trotting around the pasture where Daddy had fenced the pony in, I could see our big stucco house with the pointed lightning rods, each skewering a green glass globe, and the side porch covered with the inbred black cats that I adored. After a while, Daddy let me go beyond the pasture and ride all over the property. We didn't have money, but we did have some land, eleven acres including part of North Run Creek, some woods, and a patch of swamp where I wasn't allowed to go.

To my joy, I had all these new friends, boys and girls who showed up at my house to beg rides on the pony's cheerful spotted back. My new friends badgered me for turns, and some of them took the pony into the swamp anyway, while I shrieked for them to come back.

Who were these boys and girls? They were Val Price, of the knowing smile; Dennis Lassiter, pale and kind, always saved for last in games of dodgeball because he was plump, an "easy out"; Irvin Kitchen, handsome even as a child; gentle Jackie Bowman, so frail that Mama worried she would keel over while riding; Mary Sue Talley, of the womanly figure and furry armpits; and Rusty Satterwhite, who defied Miss Genevieve by forcing spit through his teeth as she scolded him: "You trifling *thing!*" I envied Rusty Satterwhite for living at the old hotel, which had long served as a home for families who were hardscrabble poor.

Best of all, there was Evangeline Stanback, the sheriff's granddaughter, as poised and severely beautiful as a queen. She knew how to post, her straight back moving up and down as the pony trotted. My sisters and I cheered as she posted down the driveway and urged the pony into a canter when she reached the road.

After three weeks, I went out one morning to check on the pony and he was simply gone, pasture empty, with no clues or telltale tracks. I called and called him, searching in the woods and the swamp. It was a Saturday in late May. Uncharacteristically, a morning storm broke, heavy with thunder and lightning, driving me back to the house. Celestial arms flailed great whips of rain. I climbed the steps to the attic and peered out of the highest window, hoping to see the pony loping toward me. Everything was green, even the sky, and through the drafty attic walls, I smelled sweet ozone. The rain beat on the roof so loudly that I was soothed and fell to poking in old boxes of Christmas ornaments and the closet where outgrown clothes and toys were kept. I found an old photograph stuck on a shelf. It showed a group of young women in front of a school, wearing white ruffly gowns like those of the party guests at the old hotel. In the front row, the teacher smiled a secret smile. One of the girls looked like Miss Genevieve.

When the storm was over, when the battered morning glories had raised their heads again on the pasture fence, my new friends showed up and asked, "Where is he?"

"I don't know! I was hoping some of y'all had seen him," I said.

They took off then, some in tears. I'd never heard such a slamming of doors as they leaped back into their parents' cars or jumped onto their bikes. I just had so little to hold them, without the pony.

THE OTHER episode I've never told anybody about involves two films about Alaska and Hawaii. Soon after my dawn excursion to the school, Miss Genevieve herded my classmates and me down to the fallout shelter to view these films, which she had borrowed from the Henrico County Public Library. The deep darkness of the fallout shelter made a perfect movie place. It was really just a basement, but the romance of bombs was alive in my heart in those days. I didn't comprehend the destruction bombs could do; I just loved the idea of their enormous light. After all, Miss Genevieve had seen every bone in her hand.

"Two new states," Miss Genevieve said. "Two new stars on the flag."

I knew that Alaska and Hawaii had been states for some years now, long enough for the films to get staticky. In the unearthly backglare from the projector, I saw Miss Genevieve's face, strained across the cheekbones and so tired that I knew for the first time what exhaustion really meant. With wonder and certainty, I realized she would die very soon. I sucked in my breath and hunkered down on the long wooden bench. Her death would be quick—a light cut off, a fire doused. On the screen, somebody made a shadow puppet of a rabbit: Rusty Satterwhite. The shadow blotted out a family of Eskimos snatching bits of fish from a communal bowl. When Miss Genevieve didn't reprimand him, Rusty finally yanked his arm down.

When *Alaska* ended, Miss Genevieve rewound the film and slipped it into a flat metal case. *Hawaii* was next. Along with my classmates, I was spellbound by wild teal waves, brown surfers, hibiscus-decked hula dancers, fields of pineapple, and Honolulu street scenes. The people smiled so wide, moved so fast, laughed so much.

Miss Genevieve did die, that very afternoon after school. It happened at the grocery store. I heard how she curled gracefully to the floor, a cabbage in one hand and a can of sardines in the other, swooned like a debutante curtseying, her chin touching the floor before the rest of her did. A substitute teacher inherited her beautifully penned lesson plans. The substitute couldn't get my name right; she kept calling me Linda.

I lay awake in the spring evening and thought about Miss Genevieve's desperate face in the light of the film projector. A late train rattled past, going far away. It was then that I remembered the two films in their metal cases, down in the fallout shelter: Miss Genevieve had stacked them on top of the projector. I knew I was the only one who remembered they were there.

For several days, I skipped class to watch the films. At first I had trouble setting up the projector, feeding the thin curling edge of brown film into it properly and making sure all the switches were set to "on." With every viewing I sat on a different bench, because I could get varied angles on the screen that way, and I noticed new things each time: the scar on a hula dancer's shoulder, the lopsidedness of a coconut, the sunset hues of a lei. Caribou raced across Alaskan tundra, the angry emeralds of the Northern Lights flashed above the Bering Strait, and teenagers tossed their heads and bounded down the steps of a stark new Alaskan school. Depending on where I sat, the narrator's voice changed pitch, as did the islanders' songs and the sled dogs' barking. I turned the volume up loud, louder, until my ears burned and tweeted. Every time a film ended, I enjoyed the ritual all over again, especially the swift secret hum of rewinding.

Nobody knew about this, not even Mama, whose keen intuitions should have alerted her to the sooty basement scent of my clothes and the surfers and timber wolves mirrored in my pupils. Incredibly, nobody at school heard the racket the films made down in the fallout shelter.

At last, on a dreamy, dark June afternoon, I'd had enough. I slid the films into their metal cases for a final time and returned them to the Henrico County Public Library. Back then, the library was in a huge old house located beyond everything else—past the old hotel, the post office, the grocery store, the filling station, in a patch of woods all its own, with an iron gate out front. Long ago, Captain Cussons had built it as an example of housing suitable for his village, and had rented it out to friends.

Inside, the library was all business, its Victorian rooms crammed with sleek shelves, dark wooden tables, and whispery patrons turning pages and poring over a card catalog. I'd been there many times. The stuffed owl on top of the card catalog was an old friend. I marched up to the circulation counter, films in hand, and who should be perched there, half-moon glasses slipping down his nose, but Gibby Beasley.

"So you got away with it, Swing Girl," he said with his blazing eyes and actor's grin. "I figured some schoolkid was hanging onto these movies, watching them. They're long overdue."

"Do you work here now? Are you going back to Hollywood?" I asked.

"We're in Hollywood right this second," he said. "We're on camera. Oh, I don't know. Mother asked me to stay for a while, and I needed a vacation. My brother has his hands full managing the Youth Center. Do you ever go there? I've been after him to let me set up a pool table in the pavilion. I'm a hell of a shot."

He took the film cases from me, stamped them with some device, and tossed them beneath the counter. For all I knew, he was throwing them away.

A realization hit me: school was out. That very day had been the last day. I had spent it in the rapt darkness of the fallout shelter.

"Now that school's out, I can go to the Youth Center more," I said.

"But you lost your pony," Gibby said with a mean look. "I heard about that. Mother's disgusted with you for not taking better care of it. That pony was in our yard one morning, eating irises. I should have called you."

"You should have!" I cried. People raised their heads from their books and stared at me. "When was that?"

"Weeks ago. He's still around, though, your pony. I've heard his hoofbeats on the road." To the library patrons, Gibby announced, "Closing time." He slid off his high stool and strolled out in front of the circulation desk, jingling a ring of keys. The patrons scurried out. In moments, the library was empty, the still air electrified by their presence.

"Nothing like a good book, I always say," Gibby said with a sneer.

"I love books," I said. "Why do you work here if you don't like them?" He was so short and absurd, so combative, that he invited challenge. I remembered that day on the swings: I'd flown higher than he had, higher than anybody ever had.

"Who said I don't like books?" he said. "Though I'd rather read scripts. Where are you going now?"

"Home," I said.

"So am I," he said with a sigh. "I'd go to the Youth Center, but my brother is always there, moping about his lost talent. He didn't have that much talent to begin with, never mind that he played the piano for the president when he was four years old."

We went outside, where Gibby hopped on a bike that was leaning against a trellis. He spun the pedals with his feet.

I said, "Remember that day I swung so high? I saw all of Glen Allen, even the past. It was all there—Captain Cussons and the old hotel. He was giving a party."

Gibby paused, gripping his handlebars. "Better for you if you'd seen the future," he said. "You could save yourself a lot of trouble." He rode off.

Just suppose I had seen the future? Had seen, or foreseen, that that very summer the governor's adopted daughter would be killed by lightning at Virginia Beach; that in just a year or two there'd be rock-and-roll bands playing in the parking lot of the strip shopping center, and go-go girls dancing in cages; that as a lonely teenager I would wait at the railroad tracks and record train sounds over a tape of the Beatles' *Abbey Road,* looping the tape so that I got half an hour of burning, churning, gnashing wheels and looming sad whistle music; that at the age of thirty I would watch, cringing, as the old hotel was torn down.

By then I was married and living in Richmond. As soon as I got the news of the demolition, I hurried to Glen Allen, reaching it at twilight, early enough to see how wrecked the hotel was already, late enough that as I rocked on my heels on the roadside, in the midst of the lingering construction workers, I felt afraid. I was the only woman, and there were so many men, passing a bottle around and laughing. It was a lonely road, unchanged. The same small grocery store still stood there, closed for the day, and through the woodsmoke-scented dusk the railroad tracks curved toward the vanishing point. The hotel's walls were nearly gone. Its great staircases swept unceilinged to the sky. The old oaks gave off a tidal March smell, their new leaves tiny in the cold. Had Mama been there, she would have lifted her head in the direction of the James River and said, "The shad are running."

I sprang back into my car and headed back to Richmond. My husband was impatient when I told him about the hotel being knocked down. He wanted me to take off my clothes.

If I'd seen the future, I'd have known that these days, years after its beginning, the Youth Center offers a crocodile pen where the swimming pool used to be. William Beasley's Reptiland draws bigger crowds than the dance-and-swim-and-swing playground ever did. The crocodiles never, ever seem to move. People hurl coins down onto their dark ridged backs, but they don't flinch. Quarters, dimes, and nickels glitter in the sun.

If I'd seen the future, I could have warned Gibby Beasley that he would hurt himself, though not too badly, in a fall

from a New York stage. Just the other day, I read about that
in a celebrity gossip column and heard his little leg snap like
a pretzel. He's on his fourth marriage, Gibby is. His career
lapsed for a time. I used to see him on commercials for dan-
druff shampoo, with his brushy hair divided into two equal
puffs of white suds. Now he's hot again. The newspapers always say how sexy he is, and how famous are his new wife's
breasts.

THE SUMMER that I turned eleven, my family moved to central Pennsylvania. Mama and Daddy didn't sell the Glen Allen
house, though. They rented it out to a family named Dillard,
who quit paying after a few months and were replaced by a
group of college students, then by hard-core hippies who
painted the woodwork purple and let their dogs pee on the
floor. Summer after summer, my family went down to Glen
Allen to reclaim the house, to clean up the vandalism and the
foul smells, and rent it again. Sometimes we stayed for weeks,
long enough to harvest vegetables in the overgrown garden.
Mama had a knack for finding chips of old china in the garden, evidence of some long-gone house. She kept the pieces
in a flowerpot: shards of blue delft, part of a stoneware teacup,
a sliver of pink porcelain.
    Furious at Daddy for evicting them, the departing hippies
had bashed holes in the walls, torn out a bathroom sink, and
shot out every one of the glass globes on the lightning rods.
Mama cried when she saw the damage, then went to the grocery store and bought pork chops for supper and some strong
disinfectant which she used to scour the stove. Despite our
sleeping bags on the floor and laundry washed in a plastic
wading pool out in the yard, we were home again. I found a
striped cat abandoned by the hippies and made a pet of it,

wondering what shouts, what music must have washed into its torn old ears.

I had real trouble adjusting to central Pennsylvania. The winters were horrible, I thought, endless and cold, and at school I was teased mercilessly because of my southern accent and bookish ways. Rapidly I became a hermit. When I could gain an audience, usually a shy child younger than myself, I spun tales of my glory days with the pony.

"Plus," I'd say, as my listener fidgeted and looked for escape, "my best friend, an actor, lives in Hollywood."

So I lived for those summers in Glen Allen. Despite William Beasley's melancholy and his habit of installing one upright piano after another and then banishing it as if it were the very embodiment of his lost prodigy-hood, the Youth Center flourished. My friends of the pony-riding days were growing up and going to dances at the pavilion, where garage bands twanged out love rhythms on drums and guitars. Evangeline Stanback and Irvin Kitchen embraced in sinuous sweaty movements that quickened my heart. "Jealousy, jealousy," the music seemed to cry, as I sat on a bench drinking Nehi orange, impressing Val Price and Jackie Bowman with stories of my cosmopolitan life up North. We were all fourteen then, drawing together in the warm negative communion that girls create when boys aren't asking them to dance. Val and Jackie and I had a crush on one of the drummers, a rough, good-looking sixteen-year-old named Brent Robinson, who had moved to Glen Allen from Memphis just when I'd moved away.

"He's smiling at *you*, Lyndoll," whispered Val, and it was true: I was the one Brent grinned at when he sang "Diamond Girl" and again during "I Fought the Law and the Law Won," and I was the one he kissed during the band's break, outside the pavilion.

"You oughta be part of my act," Brent Robinson said, sliding his hands beneath my blouse. I could feel the calluses on his strong fingers. "I wouldn't let you wear nothing but a boa constrictor and a hat."

"I hear you're real smart," I said, kissing his sideburns.

"Just ask me when the Franco-Prussian War was. Ask me what pitchblende is," he said, and laughed.

He smelled older than he was, a city smell that put me in mind of the Richmond that had dazzled me as a child, with its scents of fried chicken and traffic. When he laughed, he sounded tired in a sexy way, and he smoked tired too, like he was trying to stop.

He told me about Memphis. There was a bluff on the Mississippi River, he said, where he used to practice with his shotgun. It was a deserted, empty place, he said; his spent shells on the riverbank below the bluff numbered in the hundreds now, empty casings that had sounded so damn good when he fired them. We went to his car and got lost in kissing, while his band played on without him. He told me about his family. His father was crazy, he said. They had moved here so his father could take a job at Reynolds Metals downtown, but his father disliked his coworkers and showed it by wearing dark glasses to meetings and breaking wind at will. Brent's disgust about his father enthralled me.

Later, Brent drove me home, honking the horn at my parents, who sat on the side porch, though he didn't get out of the car, just rolled off into the deep darkness. Because of a June heat wave, my sisters and I dragged our sleeping bags into the upstairs hallway that night to catch the breezes, but for me it was no use. Around two in the morning, I got up and tiptoed downstairs and onto the porch.

Mama was there. "I couldn't sleep either," she said. "Look at the moon shining on the trees just like snow." She wore an old seersucker robe, and in her lap she held the flowerpot where she kept her bits of china.

"Brent asked me to meet him tomorrow night at the Youth Center," I said, wanting her approval of him.

"He looks right wild," she said. "He should have come up on the porch to meet Daddy and me, but he just let you out and drove off."

Instantly I resented those high standards of hers, the way she never allowed exceptions in men's treatment of her daughters. He was my first date, and she was finding fault with him, and she was right.

"I wish I were grown up and could live by myself," I said, wanting to hurt her feelings. I had thought such things before, but hadn't said so. My sisters would never have said that. "I figure I've got about four years left before I can be on my own, forever."

Mama's face showed surprise. In the strange light (where had I seen that light before?), I saw the shiny rims of tears in her eyes. She said, "Who'd want to be on their own forever?"

"I'm sorry," I said, kneeling beside her and catching her hand. She didn't squeeze my hand back, and I felt a choking fear.

"Let's walk," she said, setting aside the flowerpot full of china bits. I thought, Mama, you never walk around at night; even when you can't sleep, you lie in your bed.

We moved through the moonlight over the damp grass, toward the vegetable garden. "I'll help you look for china pieces," I said. Tree frogs sang in the woods and in the swamp, and heat lightning glimmered over the open fields.

Daddy had just cut the grass that day; clumps of it stuck to our feet.

As we reached the vegetable garden, something large and lighted and warlike rose in silence from the horizon. I held Mama's hand and we stood rooted amid the tomato plants, gazing. Studded with lanterns of red and gold along its great wings, the ship passed over us and beyond the forest.

"What *was* it," we asked each other, again and again, that night and all summer long.

"Some new Air Force plane, a superfast, silent kind," Daddy would say, but neither Mama nor I really wanted an explanation. Years later, when she was dying, I said, "Remember the great big quiet plane, that night in Glen Allen," and she nodded her gentle head. We hadn't spoken of it for a long time, the voyaging, secret thing.

BRENT ROBINSON didn't show up for our next date, but he had a good excuse: he'd been wrenching a gun out of his father's hands so his father wouldn't blow away the whole family. Brent did manage to get the gun, but he didn't finish growing up, because his family died in a strange fire. Val Price, my best Glen Allen correspondent during my exile in Pennsylvania, wrote me about it. On Halloween, Pa Robinson had carved a pumpkin, stuck a candle in it, and passed out drunk at the kitchen table in front of the jack-o'-lantern while the rest of the family slept upstairs. When the fire spilled out of the pumpkin and set the whole house ablaze, old Pa was the only one who got out in time. Val Price wrote me that she could smell the fire and see the last smoke on the horizon the next morning.

For years, I dreamed of that jack-o'-lantern, dreamed the smell of its flesh as the candle flared into the orange hollow and blackened the tough, seamed rind. Pa Robinson must have opened his drunken eyes and seen before him, on the red-hot kitchen table, the pumpkin's grin—those triangle eyes and crenellated teeth. Then the fire melted the pert cap of stem and burst through the eyes and mouth and nose hole: a laughing squash, a cussing head, something nurtured and made a pet of, a hydrogen bomb Pa Robinson had made, bleeding fire from its knife wounds.

Now I'm the one living in Memphis, the city Brent Robinson called home. My husband and I have separated. He's still in Richmond, but I got a job here. Sometimes, with a friend or two, I do the snazziest thing in town—go to tea at the Peabody Hotel. We savor the tiny pastries of lemon and hazelnut and the miniature sandwiches of salmon and cucumber, sitting close to the fountain where famous ducks play, ducks which, promptly at five each afternoon, are induced by a scarlet-liveried duckmaster to step out of the fountain, beat their wings, and trundle down a red carpet to the elevator. Giddy as the tourists who aim their cameras, my friends and I applaud: at that moment, this is the most important event in all of the Mid-South, these pampered ducks putting on their show. The flower arrangement on top of the ducks' fountain must weigh five hundred pounds. If it's Easter season, the lobby displays a solid chocolate duck sculpted by Peabody chefs, a ten-foot tall confection that you can smell all the way out into the street. I always think, Brent Robinson should be here at the Peabody, a rich and successful man by now, cheering the ducks with a wife and daughters wearing bright sash-tied dresses.

I have seen where the ducks spend their evenings, up on the roof in a curlicued golden hut. Guano dots the AstroTurf. From the roof, you can see the shore of Arkansas, and Beale

Street with its noisy blues beckons from just a block away. Once I watched a man with a bandaged foot strolling down the alley holding a crutch. When he reached Beale Street—which is where the tourists and conventioneers go after the ducks leave the Peabody lobby—he stuck the crutch under one arm and limped and begged. Even from the roof, way high above the city, I could see the white shine of his smile.

A FEW years before Mama died, she and Daddy decided to sell the Glen Allen house. "Our ship has come in," they said, proud of getting their price, but I thought the new owners were the lucky ones, despite the fact that all over Glen Allen by then, you could hear the traffic on Route 295. When I was growing up, how hushed it was. All you could hear were the bird calls and the occasional car passing by on Mountain Road, quiet as a sigh.

Mama called me in Memphis to tell me about the sale. She said, "A nice young couple bought it. They actually make movies."

"Do they know Gibby Beasley?" I asked, laughing.

"Documentaries, not movie-movies," Mama said.

"I miss that house," I said. "I miss you," because Mama and Daddy were still living in central Pennsylvania and were so far from Memphis. What I wanted was to walk with Mama in that vegetable garden and find pieces of china for her, and to ride the pony again.

What if my raffle pony *were* Captain Cussons's pony, the very same one that I saw in my vision of the long-ago party? By the time I was eight, the pony was at least seventy years old. His sturdy stocky self had tugged phaetons filled with generations of children; boys and girls perched on his spotted back, hugging him, naming him different names. He wore out his saddles. He ground his iron shoes to powder. His riders grew up and died. By the time I came along and won him in Mrs. Beasley's raffle, no wonder he was restless, ready to melt away into his own hoofbeats on Mountain Road, the flat Tidewater road two hours from any hills and one hour from the sea, galloping west, galloping east, with the Captain's rose garden a sweet red riot in his memory, and no more children's heels against his sides.

Snow Day

I.

NELLE FENTON WAS in Florida visiting John, the oldest of her seven sons, when she received the terrible news that her youngest boy, Dudley, had eloped with Nelle's housekeeper. The woman, Mildred Murphy, was low-class, in Nelle's opinion, and she was more than twenty years older than Dudley: seventy-three or four to Dudley's fifty. The elopement was only technical. They had not run away. After a visit to the justice of the peace at the county courthouse, they had returned to Nelle's Virginia farmhouse, where Dudley lived also.

It was New Year's Day when Dudley called to tell her about this marriage.

"Take that woman and go," Nelle ordered Dudley, while John and his wife Harriet paced nearby, extracting the news from Nelle's side of the conversation. "I don't want either of you there when I get back."

Nelle handed the receiver to John and went outside to the half-dozen citrus trees that John and Harriet called the grove: two each of lemon, orange, and lime. Dudley had said, "I have some news, Mother, good news," yet he must have known she would be outraged. Nelle reached up and touched the hanging fruits. They were never as brilliantly colored as they should be. She tore a lime from a branch and held it to her nose. The skin was not green, but a leathery yellow, and it smelled harsh. Nelle had been in Lake Worth for only a few days, yet already Christmas in Virginia seemed long ago. Her daughters-in-law had assembled Christmas dinner, for Mildred Murphy had declared she didn't feel well and had taken to her bed. Now Nelle saw that for the ploy it was. She remembered Dudley hovering furtively in the hallway near Mildred's room. Oh, she'd known about their doings. She'd planned to fire Mildred as soon as she could find somebody else. It wasn't easy hiring a housekeeper. That slattern was worse than nobody, though. On the job two months. On the make with Dudley.

Nelle's mouth was completely dry, her heart wild.

She squeezed the lime until it burst between her fingers. Harriet came out of the house and said, "Oh, Mother F! Here, let's go inside," as if it were cold, as if they were in a Virginia snowfall instead of this strange place with its sultry sun. Through the glass patio doors, Nelle saw John hang up the phone. She threw the mutilated lime to the ground and allowed Harriet to escort her back into the house. Harriet always dressed coquettishly, in tight dresses and high heels, unless she were flying, copiloting the Cessna with John, in which case she became Amelia Earhart, in slacks, goggles, and scarves. They were childless, Harriet and John.

Nelle recalled that Mildred Murphy had offspring from some earlier marriage or liaison. Such women always did, and grandchildren too, garrulous, pitiful, threatening creatures who would slobber over Dudley, demanding money from him the rest of their lives. Nelle would ban them all from her house. She would get another dog. Yes, a ferocious one to live on the porch. Her poodles were for indoors, though they were not exactly friendly to strangers.

And Dudley was her favorite son. Had been. Until now.

"Let's sit down and have some orange juice," Harriet said. She took a carton from the refrigerator and poured juice into small glasses. John pulled out a chair for Nelle—a tiny, silly chair made of metal, with a red plastic seat—and she sat down. Their furniture belonged in a garden or an ice-cream parlor, though John had retired a wealthy man from his airplane hangar business. He and Harriet put their money into cars, a new Cadillac for each. They took the house and the tiny citrus grove and themselves very seriously. Nelle didn't think Harriet was sorry there were no children. John, maybe. He would have been a good father, never mind that he was twice divorced, Harriet his third wife.

"Mother F, what will you do?" Harriet said.

"Dudley said he doesn't want you to feel bad," said John. "Said they'll live with one of her daughters until they can find a place of their own."

They drank the juice. Nelle's hands stank of the lime she had mangled. Mildred Murphy's image came to her—greasy hair, glazed gaze. "She has cataracts," Nelle announced.

"To think," Harriet sputtered, "that they would do this, and behind your back." Harriet was delighted by the chance to prove her allegiance to Nelle. Rivalry among daughters-in-law was normally something Nelle relished, but she could take no pleasure in Harriet's show of loyalty.

John's face went slack, his lower lip pendulous. Had he had a stroke? This was how horrors happened, not one at a time but in swift succession. John's hand trembled. Then he reached for the carton and poured another glass of juice, and Nelle breathed again. Her oldest boy was just getting old.

John said, "He must have been drinking. I didn't ask him. I didn't have to."

"Mildred is rather dreadful," said Harriet.

How like Harriet to point out the obvious. Nelle's thoughts were moving ahead of them to a point of resolve. She was in a war that she hadn't seen coming, and everything she said and did at this critical time would be reported by John and Harriet to her other sons and their wives.

"I need to get back home," she said.

John nodded. "We'll go as soon as you're ready." He would have the Cessna prepared, would hand Nelle's bags up to Harriet, see that they were settled, and bend to the controls of the plane with a mind that Nelle knew to be blank except for the necessities of flying. The thought of that blankness comforted her. It had always been airplanes and women for John, and cars.

Suddenly, Nelle couldn't wait to get home, no matter that it would be icy and bleak all through January. It would still be beautiful, with deep snow around the fences and cedars, the air cold and silent and smelling of wood smoke.

She could figure this out, about Dudley and this woman.

John and Harriet waited. They could tell there was something else. Nelle reached for her cane, rolling her palm over it as she sat there in her silly chair, almost ninety years old, a thousand miles from her house. Even now, the woman and Dudley were defying her. They might go back to bed, in Dudley's room, knowing it would be at least tomorrow before Nelle could return. Or maybe Nelle's own bed—but Dudley wouldn't, even drunk, no matter what the old broad might say, wheedling, opening her dress.

On Christmas Day, when Mildred had stayed abed, Nelle had ordered her to call someone to come for her if she were ill, and the woman had replied, "All their phones are cut off." Planning it then, with Dudley stealthy in the hall. Folly to leave them together, though the woman had lied that she'd be going to a daughter's house the day Nelle departed.

"Mother F," said Harriet, "shall I help you pack?" Harriet's face was so strained, Nelle was tempted to say, "Oh, go on and cry," for Harriet was prim and dramatic. John would be busy the rest of the day, tending his mother and his wife.

Nelle decided she wouldn't need any tending. She rapped her cane on the floor. "I will outlive her," she said, and their heads snapped up.

"WELL. GEE," said Davy Dalton.

We had a deal. I wrote his papers for him; he listened to my stories. Since my own life was boring, I resorted to episodes from my grandmother's past. She was the most dashing person I knew. The words, the feeling for her adventures, which I'd heard more from other family members than from my grandmother herself, would bubble up in my soul, only to come clunking out of my mouth like pieces of chalk. My grandmother and Dudley and Mildred lived eighty miles to the west in farm country which seemed farther away than it really was.

I had begged Davy for this arrangement: "Just give me a chance." To make him love me, I meant. I had loved him for so long, ever since he moved to Glen Allen in the third grade.

Recently, there had been assignments on heraldry and foreign currency. I'd written terrific papers for him on those topics. This one, for our eighth-grade health class, was on head lice. He got B+'s on the forged papers. He would never get A's, simply because the papers said Davy Dalton at the top.

I copied the final draft onto clean paper, slanting my writing so it resembled his backhand. "Now ask," I said. He was required to ask three questions about each of my tales.

Davy sighed. We sat at his kitchen table, which bore scabs of dried scrambled eggs. To kiss him, I would have to back him into a corner. There were too many doors in his kitchen. At any minute, his sister or brother or parents might burst in. Even in a corner, it wouldn't be safe to kiss, and he'd never seemed to want to kiss me.

"Okay," Davy said. "What's a Cessna? A plane?"

"Yes, a little bitty one. My Uncle John likes to fly it. Aunt Harriet can fly, too."

Davy yawned. Wouldn't my sophistication win him? Did he understand this scandal for what it was? The charwoman, my mother called Mildred.

"So did she outlive that other lady?"

"My grandmother's fine. Mildred is still around, but she's sick a lot. My grandmother forgave my uncle Dudley, but she still won't let Mildred in the house."

Davy reached for the essay, saying, "Lemme write my name on it."

I jerked it away from him, holding it high. "You have to ask one more question."

Again he sighed, and I knew a fear that other men would sigh and want me to leave.

"So is everybody in your family like, really old? How come your grandmother is ninety-something? My grammaw's not nearly that old."

"I'm proud she's old. People can have babies when they're in their forties. Anyway, that's not a good question. Don't you see," I said. "It was all about sex. Seduction."

I threw the paper on the table. Davy smiled. "That's a right good story, Edie."

"You could ask a thousand questions about that story, if you bothered to be curious. As a matter of fact, I think my uncle's pretty happy with Mildred."

Davy blinked. He had his mother's eyes, capable of great grief. I feared his mother. She worked at the post office, and during her breaks she stood outside in the parking lot, smoking hard. Davy said, "I bet you're gonna be a teacher. You act like one."

I played my ace. My grandmother had raised horses until she grew too old to ride, and I knew a little of the lore. "Do you know what to do if you're riding a horse and it bolts?"

"You mean, like this?" Davy slapped his palms together in a sliding motion.

"You ride in a spiral, in littler circles till you get to the middle, and then it'll stop."

"Okay," Davy said. He laughed at me.

I tried to slam the door as I went out, but it was a humid October night, and the swollen door stuck in its frame. In the Daltons' dark backyard, a mosquito shrilled. Being at their house was a great risk. I had told my mother I would be at Cathy Collier's house, when in fact Cathy Collier and I hadn't been friends since the fifth grade. I went home.

"Don't think of her as some grand, romantic figure," my mother once said to me about my grandmother, her mother-in-law. "She exaggerates everything. She's very selfish."

And gets away with it, I could have said, as I intended to get away with it.

II.

Years went by. Davy Dalton's mother, Janice, was still working at the post office. There she'd be in the parking lot, smoking cigarettes on her breaks. By then I was seventeen, and I knew my life would be better than Janice's, that my face wouldn't look as if I'd always been crying. Davy was still in school, but he took dummy math and dummy English, the kind kids took when they had no plans for college. He'd had many girlfriends. His steady was a pretty pop-eyed blonde whose family attended the same church mine did. Her daddy owned a car dealership.

Davy was a commotion in the hallway, a topic of gossip, his name a whoop on girls' lips. He even broke the hearts of girls who had graduated and were working as cashiers and bank tellers, grownups who should have known better than to mess with him.

One day I went to the post office to mail a letter, on foot, though I had my driver's license by then. Sometimes it was easier to walk rather than to argue with my mother that I was a safe driver. I dropped the letter in the box—it was a birthday card for my grandmother. As the metal box clacked, Janice looked up and called to me.

"Edie! I remember you. You used to help Davy," she said, "with his papers."

"Oh, he didn't need much help," I said, my old loyalty surging back.

I realized Janice knew I wrote the papers myself. "Come see us," she said.

It was a raw day, getting on to darkness. She was younger than I am now, yet she seemed old and finished, the way I was too old by then for Davy, and through with him.

Except I wasn't. Davy's scarred boots clattering down the high school steps, the back of his curly head glimpsed through the door of the shop studio—thoughts of him came to me one morning soon after I'd seen his mother. There had been a heavy snow, and school was closed. For one day, time would stand still.

I went to the Daltons' house, praying Davy was there by himself, counting on that, for I was on a mission—to lose my virginity. When he answered the door, he grinned, deep and sly. He needed to shave, but I didn't care. My mission took only fifteen minutes in Davy's room, his bed. Davy was so accustomed to sex. Already, he had his own patterns, which he explained as we proceeded: "Now you do this, and I'll go like this." His voice was matter-of-fact.

Afterwards, we watched TV in the den. Then, with a great bumbling and clatter at the door, his father came home sick from his job at a cabinet factory, acting not the least bit surprised to find me there—a girl unknown to him. "Could you fix me some tea?" he said, sneezing. I did, and he accepted a mug from my hand as if he'd done that a million times.

The man's exhaustion registered on me. I saw that this was an ordinary day to him, that in a few weeks or months he would not remember coming home early. That was how it would be with a husband—a man coming home, expecting to find you in his house where you belonged, not even looking up as he took a mug of tea from your hand.

"That mug is chipped," I said, trying to make him glance at me. "Don't cut your mouth."

"Oh, it's fine," he said.

"Do you want sugar? Or honey? That's good for a cold."

"No, that's okay," he said.

Davy's little brother and sister came home from playing in the snow, cheeks red, asking for lunch. Before I knew it, I was heating up canned ravioli and dishing the food out to them on the only plates I could find, paper ones creased and linty from the drawer where Janice kept kitchen towels and packets of ketchup. Davy took the pot off the stove and went to eat the rest of the ravioli in front of the TV. There wasn't any left for me.

Davy's little brother asked me to mend his shirt. It was too thin, but it was the brightest color I'd seen all winter. He had ravioli on his chin. I found a needle and thread and patched the shirt. These people would keep me busy for the rest of my life. Janice didn't get home from the post office until after dark. She looked lively, as if whatever sorrow had assailed her in the parking lot was gone.

"You and Davy doing homework?" she asked with a tight smile. She knew about the sex. "Stay for supper," she said.

I did stay. Called my mother, again with my alibi of being at Cathy Collier's house. During a meal of Spaghettios and raisin bread, Davy's little brother fell asleep, his sister tried to paint my fingernails, Davy wouldn't look me in the eye, and his mother talked about shutters. Davy's father didn't eat with us. He was somewhere in the back of the house, coughing.

That cough worried me. It was deep and harsh.

"Green," Janice was saying. "Green shutters, because this house is red. Don't you think so, Edie?"

I said, "I think your husband might be really sick. He's gotten worse just since I've been here. He ought to go to the doctor."

Janice looked up sharply, as if accused. "He's fine." She paused. "You're the only girl at the school named Edith," she said, light as a slap.

"It's a family name," I said. Her husband coughed again, and a voice in my head said, Get out. Get out before you catch it, too.

Janice stared at me, her face a dare: You're in our midst. Explain yourself.

I told Janice that green shutters would be nice. Before I went home, I washed all of the dishes. Nobody thanked me or said goodbye when I let myself out the door. I knew I was not pregnant. It had felt good, what Davy and I had done together—the embraces, the clumsy connecting—good enough that I wanted to repeat it, though the wish wasn't urgent.

Overnight, the snow melted. I escaped Mr. Dalton's illness. But something had started in me, a welter of concern not for Davy but for his father, whose feverish fingers had brushed mine as I handed him the chipped mug of tea. I couldn't remember his face except for the dull fear in his eyes, the look people have when they know they're getting sick.

Davy wasn't at school the day after the snow day. At lunchtime I called his house, using the pay phone at school. Davy answered. "Yello?" he said, and I knew he'd picked that up from his mother, that Janice would be a yello person too.

"It's Edie," I said. "I wanted to know if . . ." and my voice trailed off. I didn't know how to say it, this worry about his father.

"If we can do it again?" Davy asked. "Sometime, sure. I'm busy today. My dad's sick, remember, and Mom made me stay home with him." In the background, I heard the TV.

"Could I talk to him?" I asked.

Davy was silent for a long time. "You're crazy," he said. "That's what my mom said." He hung up.

Mr. Dalton had severe bronchitis, I learned from the school grapevine. So I took food to their house and left it on the back porch, food I bought with my allowance or fixed when my mother wasn't home, so that she wouldn't know I'd made a double batch of stew or brownies, serving half to our family and toting the rest to the Daltons. My obsession grew, never mind that Mr. Dalton was forty-eight and I was seventeen. I stood outside the Daltons' house at night, in the dark, until Janice called my parents to come get me. Mr. Dalton never came out of his house, all those evenings when I stood across the street and stared up at the windows or crouched in the backyard, my chin resting on my knees. It wasn't a crush. I was afraid he would die. I was the only one who could save him, and I did it by watching over him, in the long spring of senior year. There were conferences at school involving my parents and the principal, and on those evenings, I stayed home and worked on college applications. I wrote about helping a family get rid of head lice, about leaving food for them anonymously. The essay worked: I got into William and Mary.

But it wasn't Mr. Dalton who died. By graduation day he was recovered, hale and hearty, and I could relax about him. A few days later, Davy was playing in a softball game at my church. He ran backwards, reaching for a pop fly, showing off for the big-eyed blonde, who by then was known to be pregnant with his baby and who sat in the top row of the bleachers, shielding her eyes against the hard white sky that foretold a thunderstorm. A lightning bolt flashed so close I blinked, and thunder sounded deep as the peal of a giant bell.

Davy crumpled onto the grass. While people raced toward him, his girlfriend stayed on the bleachers. Then some realization hit her, and she crawled down the risers. He'd been struck by lightning. Rain started, heavy and drenching.

Later, as my mother iced a cake for the Dalton family, I said, "Davy doesn't even go to our church. He was there because of his girlfriend."

My mother had used a mix for the cake, though she disparaged mixes. A mix meant the Daltons were beneath her. "Here, take this over to them."

"I can't." I could never take food to the Daltons again.

The lightning storm that had killed Davy had ushered in a cold front, so my mother put on her coat before she went out, her eyes meeting mine in the hall mirror. The cake's almond-flavored icing, at least, was made from scratch. Once I was alone, I would lick the bowl.

Rumors were flying, and it seemed that they reached me even as I sat in the kitchen, eating the sweet white icing: *Davy's girlfriend lost the baby. Davy predicted his own death that very morning, in a joke. Four out of five people struck by lightning are potheads, because pot attracts electricity.* Davy was a pothead; that was the only part that was true.

Davy's girlfriend gave birth to a daughter. Now that the daughter is grown, people ask them, "Are y'all sisters?" and the identical blondes smile, their eyes blue globes. They run the car dealership together. Sales are in the millions, the gazillions. You'll glimpse the yellow heads out on the car lot in all weather, see the sapphire eyes streak by on test drives. I've heard the daughter laugh, and it's Davy's chuckle coming out of her mouth. I've seen her run backwards to catch a set of car keys her mother throws her, just a step or two, but I know where the girl got that heedless reverse sprint. She wears high scarred boots when the weather turns cold: Davy's, though I can't be sure.

My grandmother died just before I left for college, and her house and land and all her prized barns were amicably sold by my father and his brothers. My uncle Dudley took her dogs home with him, the single surviving poodle and a mastiff which had shown up on the property one day and for which my grandmother had real affection. "I need company," Dudley said as he led the dogs away.

III.

By senior year at William and Mary, I was engaged to a boy who was so rich, his parents were building him his own clinic, where presumably he would join his father in practice as soon as he finished med school. First, of course, he had to get into medical school. That was his worry, not mine. I hardly thought about Chuck except on Friday nights, when he'd pull up behind my sorority house in his new sports car, ready for me to go to a motel with him. I'd be waiting, my suitcase packed, a hard-sided Samsonite of my mother's. A pocket in the suitcase was stained with dried red nail enamel, my mother's, from some excursion she had taken during World War II. I pointed it out to Chuck, hoping he'd ask for the story, but he just shrugged.

My sorority took up lots and lots of my time. During Rush Week, in September, I invented a skit: I was a surgeon, with a flashlight tied to my head, saying to rushees: "If you want to join any sorority but this one, you ought to have your brain examined," at which point my roommate, lying on her bed, rolled her eyes and flopped out her tongue. I reached under her pillow and lifted up a handful of raw ground beef. Rushees screamed. We got the best pledge class in history.

Chuck was short and fat. By spring, I'd had all the candle-light ceremonies that Chi Omega could give me—one for getting pinned, one for getting lavaliered, another for getting engaged. Spring already, yet the only med school that had accepted Chuck was one on a Caribbean island, for frauds, for quacks, people too dumb to get into a real medical school. Chuck did not despair. His parents would build the clinic no matter what, and a string would be pulled on his behalf, some string he didn't have to concern himself with.

In spring semester, I developed a habit of detaining people on the graceful staircase inside the Chi O house. I, who had always been quiet, changed into somebody who was adept at not letting people go. I told myself that I would talk just until time for class, would give myself a few minutes to rush to the lecture hall, yet with an audience caught in my snare—a pledge, a cleaning lady, a friend ready to renounce me for my capacity to block and bore—I went on and on. My diamond engagement ring was so heavy I could hardly lift my hand from the banister. Girls couldn't resist the ring, were stranded, blinded by it, while my monologue made them late for class, dates, club meetings, job interviews. I knew I was becoming a joke, that girls commiserated about me.

Yet as long as I was on the steps, stalling, it couldn't be Friday evening with Chuck waiting; it had to be a weekday, a weeknight, with time standing still. I told again the stories of my grandmother, and more of them came back to me. She had been bitten by a copperhead in her garden, had raised her arm with the snake still hanging. Her doctor was summoned.

He ordered her to drink coffee and walk up and down her yard, so as not to fall asleep. Sleep after a snakebite would be deadly.

I shook my arm, invisible snake attached, and girls covered their mouths in horror. I told about my uncle Dudley and his elopement, and the long war that played out in the midst of the family.

And Davy Dalton and the papers I wrote for him: I explained about making conversation with his mother about shutters. I was clever enough to ask my listeners an occasional question: have you ever seen a person get hit by lightning? That story made impatient listeners become, for a moment, rapt. None of them had gone to the high school Davy and I had attended. His unusual demise, though word of it had probably appeared in newspapers all across Virginia, was not anything they remembered.

To speak of my grandmother's troubles or my uncle's choice of a wife or Davy's death was to trespass on graves, yet I told myself that what I felt was daring, not shame.

BEING ENGAGED to Chuck meant spending a lot of time with his mother, she of a Cape Buffalo hairdo and lined clothing, every garment lined with silk or satin, a genteel armor. She took me to brunch, just the two of us, at the Cascades or the Williamsburg Inn, and wrote out for me Chuck's favorite recipe: a dip made with cream cheese, dried beef, green pepper, and curry, which you wouldn't think would be good but was in fact delicious. She took me shopping in Richmond, at Miller and Rhoads and at Thalhimer's, set up a bank account for me with a monthly allowance, and confided in me about interviewing potential secretaries for her husband, the challenges of choosing the ugliest one who was nonetheless competent. "It does no good," she declared, hunched over the wheel of her Mercedes. "He could fall in love with a toad."

I lined up six girls to serve as my bridesmaids. Chuck's family, not mine, was paying for the wedding, at his mother's insistence. Twice I got out of the motel weekends by pleading early-morning fittings for my wedding gown.

My arms were longer than Chuck's. That bothered me. Yet the sex was at least as good as my initiation with Davy Dalton had been, a million years earlier. And I loved the continental breakfasts at the motels where we stayed—free doughnuts and coffee. Sometimes, there were iced pastries every bit as good as the dessert table at the Cascades brunch. Chuck gained weight. He would have his tux let out, he announced.

I despaired. The Chi Omegas had given me all they could. There were no more candlelights that I qualified for. There was nothing to do but join his mother's garden club and start drinking. Spring Break came and went. Still, it was only March, the balmy Tidewater spring that lured girls to the roofs of dorms and sorority houses to start their tans. Only March: it was weeks, months even, until graduation and my June wedding. I cut class to go shopping, writing checks on Chuck's mother's money for silver bracelets and fresh fudge. Chuck's mother took me to her dermatologist, who got rid of my freckles once and for all.

Meanwhile, my roommate fell in love with a man who came to fix our ceiling fan. She moved out and married him. By then it was April, but there were still faculty teas to go to, the Pan-Hellenic Easter egg hunt, and the annual Spring Fling, which required the mixing of gallons of alcoholic punch in new plastic garbage cans. As long as there were events, rituals, I was safe. I had time. Chuck buzzed around me lackadaisically, a slow, fat fly that wouldn't mind being swatted. I said so to my sorority sisters. Suddenly I was funny. That was Chuck's gift to me, others' laughter. I confessed that I'd wondered if Chuck would let me squeeze the blackheads on his nose. The girls howled. And did he? they asked. "Yes," I said, "he's like an old pet." Even as I made fun, I could have wept for how short his forearms were, how childlike his cries during nightmares. He dreamed about leaving things inside patients after surgery: a towel, a pair of scissors.

Beach Week: Chuck was out of town, interviewing at a med school where his parents had pulled a string. Five girls piled into my Pinto and headed for Virginia Beach, where we shared a room at the Mar-Jac. I stayed out all night dancing with sailors from the Navy base, got back to the room at dawn, and lay down on the only available space on the floor. The carpet smelled of old socks. Outside, waves heaved on the sand. Only a final wine-and-cheese party stood between me and commencement, after which there would be a decorous reception at the sorority house for parents, grandparents, and siblings, and then my life would be over.

My married, pregnant former roommate graduated with honors, striding across the stage beaming, rumored to be naked beneath her black crepe gown. Back at the house, during that decorous reception, I locked myself in my room and turned on the TV. A hurricane was brewing in the Atlantic. I lay back on my bed with the windows open, the hot, still air all around me. My wedding gown was waiting at the best bridal shop in Norfolk, enough tulle and lace to clothe a parade of fairy queens. I turned the sound off the TV and watched a diagram of the hurricane swirl silently across the screen: my wedding dress, white and spinning. The storm would hit the coast that very night, flattening the new clinic Chuck's parents were building for him.

By day's end, my parents had packed my things into my Pinto and their Pontiac. We would caravan. They were outside the sorority house waiting for me. The house was empty except for Chuck and me. We sat on the sofa in the living room, which looked so small, I couldn't imagine how the entire sorority had ever held meetings there, much less the candlelight ceremonies at which I was the star. "I just don't love you," Chuck said. I took off the ring and handed it to him, heavy as a lock. Outside, my father honked the horn. Chuck stood up and walked out the door. I had ridden my runaway horse in a spiral, making the circles tighter and tighter, until stopping dead center. Daddy was honking the horn, and time had run out.

My parents announced they were hungry, so we would go out to eat. Every restaurant around Williamsburg overflowed with graduates and their families—the fancy sit-down places, the cafeterias, the seafood shacks, the hamburger stands—so we drove all the way to Richmond and stopped at a new eatery decorated to look like a barn, the walls festooned with hoes and scythes and lanterns. The waiters and waitresses wore denim overalls, calico shirts, and straw hats. "Old Mac-Donald" played on loudspeakers. We sipped ice water from Mason jars.

"This is silly," my father said.

My mother sometimes answered him in bird calls. That day she was a cardinal. "Ceedric, ceedric, ceedric," she caroled, and ordered roast beef from the startled waiter. We all did: roast beef with mashed potatoes.

My mother was convinced that the food we were served, which took so long to arrive, was not roast beef but horse meat.

She would fuss about horse meat for that entire summer, when I felt my life was over because I was still living at home with my parents and the only job I could find was selling shoes at the department store where Chuck's mother had canceled my charge account.

"Horse meat," my mother said that evening at the barn-style restaurant, her face white as she poked at the food on her plate. "This gravy doesn't fool me." She cast a furious eye at the washboards and feed buckets suspended from the walls and ceiling. I told my parents about the broken engagement. My mother said, "You didn't love Chuck, so you haven't lost anything."

My father said, "Jean, that's not true. She did lose something." To me, he said, "Your mother and I are getting a divorce. We wanted you to get through exams before we told you."

"Oh," I said, my stomach numb. Divorce.

"What'll you do next?" my father asked.

"I don't know," I said.

My mother said, "You'll dream the dream everybody has after they graduate, about being late for a test."

She was right, of course. In that dream, I wander lost in the Sunken Garden, the emerald-green expanse in the center of campus. I tell my mother about that dream, now that I'm forty-five and she's almost eighty, and she says, "You can't get lost in the Sunken Garden. It's just a great big rectangle of grass, with trees around it."

"It's a dream," I say.

Sometimes she still responds in bird calls, and now I can't tell if it's her illness or the sense of humor that was always sharper and more oblique than anybody else's, as keen as her sense of grievance. "Pee-wee," she says.

"Mama," I say, "you know I love you."

My tiny poison heart has opened up, and my mother is there in the center of it, she and my father.

THAT NIGHT at the barn restaurant, she said to my father and me, "Eat this meat at your own peril."

My father signaled the waiter, who wiped his hands nervously on his overalls as he approached our table. "My wife wants to send her food back to the kitchen," my father said. "She thinks it's horse meat."

The waiter's mouth fell open. He sputtered, "Oh, no sir, no ma'am, it's prime beef."

"Never mind," my mother said, pushing her plate away. "You can dump this out the back door for varmints to eat. I don't care. But I would like some dessert."

"It's on the house." The waiter's scared little smile made me want to hug him.

"Bring me some pie," my mother said, in a voice that indicated many things—decent pie was probably not available in this establishment; pie was something you could reach for when you had been persecuted and duped. The waiter brought a slice of butterscotch pie for each of us. My mother pronounced it gelatinous and set down her fork, but my father and I ate all of ours.

My mother would tell the story of the horse meat a hundred times in the years to come, her indignation flourishing. That meal was every injustice ever done to her. The ornamental washboards and feed buckets found their place in her tales, and the waiter who wiped his hands on his overalls— ". . . those filthy jeans," she said.

She and my father stayed together. After the horse meat episode, divorce was never mentioned again. What saved that marriage? At thirteen, writing essays for Davy Dalton, I could have figured it out. At twenty-one, with class starting in seven minutes, I could have explained it to my restless audience, some sweet-natured girl from Poquoson or Wytheville, or a sophisticate from Alexandria or Arlington, before my captive broke free and dashed out the door. Girls must have groaned with relief, escaping me, heaving great exhalations as they crossed Richmond Road, then beelining toward the Sunken Garden, long as a football field, smelling of crape myrtle and boxwood. You looked up through the trees on its embankments and glimpsed people rushing by, while the garden was hushed, its thick turf muffling sounds. Maybe my sorority sisters lingered there, seizing a long afternoon.

I'm not like that any more. I'd rather do anything than delay somebody. You have to work now to make me say more than a few words. That's what happens: you grow older, and your brain feels like a lump of ground beef lifted from your pillow. For a long time, my sorority sisters and I would call each other up and say, "I don't know what to do with myself." What we meant was, *My husband's having an affair,* or *I'm pregnant again,* or *I just can't stand it anymore,* and a rescue plan would be figured out: lunch and shopping. Or we'd go over to St. John's Church, where Patrick Henry made his speech, and we'd knock back a sherry and do gravestone rubbings, calling out, "Give me liberty or give me death." Then we'd head back to the Fan District or Windsor Farms and get out the Jack Daniels, never mind that it was five o'clock in the afternoon, with husbands and families needing our attention. Always five o'clock at a beautiful house, and heat lightning in the sky and rain on dark streets by the time I got in my car to go home.

It was way too close to the life Chuck's mother had planned for me. All that was missing was Chuck, who skipped med school, went into politics, and is now a big-time legislator, so neutral on issues that he's reelected time and again. "Aren't you sorry, Edie?" the girls used to ask me, only half teasing. "Sorry you let him go?"

That was our twenties, our thirties, and then I dropped out.

So I tend to my mother. I'm about half the age my grandmother was when she started on the great war of her life. I have no children. Won't ever get a call from a son saying, "I have some news, Mother. Good news."

"I knew all along she would win," I used to tell my sorority sisters, there on the steps. I hoped they would ask: How long did her hands smell of that lime she squeezed? Did she get a dog for her porch? What kind? That war with her daughter-in-law, did it mean as much to her by the time she won it?

Now I could answer them. Her hands smelled like lime forever. The gray mastiff limped up her long driveway and decided he was home, and she loved him so much, it changed her heart. And the war, well, for all I know, in her last days she called it off.

CPSIA information can be obtained
at www.ICGtesting.com
Printed in the USA
LVOW03s0515121017
552131LV00001B/4/P